L(
Grafton Street

Love in Grafton Street

Una Brady

BROOKSIDE

Dublin

Love in Grafton Street
is published in 1995 by
Brookside
2 Brookside
Dundrum Road
Dublin 14

ISBN 1 873748 02 7

Photo courtesy of George McCullagh
Cover Design by Brand X
Typeset by Graphic Resources
Printed in Ireland by Colour Books Ltd.

For Pat Kavanagh

VICKY sensed that the worst had happened. As the doctor in his white coat continued talking, she threw her car keys on a medicine trolley and brushed past him. Still in her night robe, she stopped for a disbelieving second before the wheel-stretcher, then threw her arms about her mother, Linda. The swing doors closed behind her and two nurses who had been in attendance retreated to wait in the corridor. Vicky cradled her mother's head and wept bitterly. Was it really true that God had taken the mother who had always cared for her, her only parent since the age of ten? As her cries filled the little room, Vicky looked at the rapidly paling face. If her mother had suffered abandonment when Vicky was a little girl, it seemed Vicky was now to be visited by the very same demon.

By now the doctor who had broken the news to Vicky had returned. He knew all about the importance of detachment, but could not bear the awful despair of this petite creature. Two nurses had also returned. One in particular, a very young nurse, was visibly upset. She belied her calmness by fixing blinds that needed no fixing, repeatedly wiping an imaginary speck of dust from her eye with a white tissue. Vicky was now running a hand up and down the sleeve of her mother's night-dress as if to keep her warm. Finally the doctor spoke, "Can we contact your father?"

An agonised shrug of Vicky's shoulders suggested he had moved into tricky territory. Had the doctor been on Linda's ward for the past three weeks, he might have twigged that she had had one faithful visitor only, Vicky herself, who stayed at the bedside for hours on end.

Vicky could not remember the exact day her father walked out, but other memories of early childhood she could recall. Her favourite, yet saddest, recollection was of a park where everything was green, where the ten-year-old had held her father's hand. On these delicious outings, she could run, tumble and scamper with abandon, knowing that fatherly eyes surveyed the scene and observed her antics with love and laughter. She would fling herself into his strong arms to be hugged, kissed and thrown up on his shoulder. Then at a signal from an antiquated music box, a race to the ice cream van. Vicky had adored him for the sense of safety she had experienced with him. All things might fall into chaos, but Daddy was predictable and reliable. Then one such Sunday, that world ended. Father put Vicky on the park bench and sat beside her, his head nudging hers. "Vicky, darling, I'm going away for some time. I will be back often to see you. I don't want you to be lonely, and remember to be good for your mother..."

Vicky had thought something in his throat prevented him from speaking further. Her childish mind put away most thoughts of sadness, but certain things couldn't be hidden, her father 'forgetting' so often to tuck in his little princess, the more frequent absences, the mysterious conversations of her parents that often ended in raised voices, and most of all the sadness of her mother. Vicky remembered the overflow of joy that possessed her when she saw her father's car outside the school. Yet now that was occurring only at intervals. Having dinner without her father at the table was absolutely horrible. And if she did ask when was her dad coming home, her mother would draw Vicky to her and press her to her heart. Try as she might, Linda could not prevent Vicky from knowing she was crying. Eventually Vicky stopped asking because the questions seemed to cause her mother such pain. And, after a while, her father's absence itself gradually inflicted less misery than before.

When Vicky was fifteen years of age, Linda explained how Walter had fallen for a legal secretary in his office. Both now lived in Munich. Linda outlined her feelings for her estranged husband. "Vicky, I still love your father. I still wear his ring. May God forgive him, and that evil woman who took him from me." She burst into tears as Vicky held her, a moment that was printed indelibly on Vicky's mind. As Vicky grew up, mother and daughter became close friends, but the topic was rarely raised. Vicky noticed that Walter's photo still took pride of place on the neat parlour cabinet, having replaced an earlier one of the newly wedded couple. That photo was now in Linda's room by her bedside. It was there since their final separation.

Linda had prayed daily that Vicky would never know the pain of break-up, though she loved to see Vicky enjoy herself. For her part, Vicky enjoyed her mother's appraisal of her appearance before she went on a date, and Linda was well aware of her twenty-year old daughter's attractiveness. Returning home at night, Vicky always saw the comforting glow of Linda's bedside lamp visible from the gravel driveway. Linda liked to read the daily newspaper from cover to cover, and although she dozed as the paper slipped in disarray over the quilt, she came wide awake at the prospect of hearing every detail of Vicky's night out. A breathless Vicky would kick off her shoes, fling herself back on the end of the bed, and if it happened to be a weekend, the clink of milk bottles was often the mutually understood signal that a few hours' sleep were now in order.

Then without warning tragedy had struck. Linda had neglected a flu, only for pneumonia to set in, leading to sudden cardiac arrest. Within weeks the angel of death had whisked away Vicky's mother, and best friend.

A few days after her mother's funeral, Vicky summoned up enough courage to enter the empty room. She opened the wardrobe and ran her hand lovingly along the various garments. Linda had always had good taste in clothes, which Vicky could not now disturb. Picking up a newspaper almost four weeks old, she folded it, remembering then that Linda's spectacles were still on the parlour cabinet, where she had brought them from the hospital. Vicky got them and returned to the bedroom. Opening the case, she caressed the spectacles, then slumping back onto her mother's bed, once more fell into uncontrollable weeping. Gently replacing the spectacles in their case, she placed it on the bedside table near Linda's reading lamp.

The photo of the newly-weds at Linda's bedside next attracted Vicky's attention. It seemed strange that Linda should keep it there, thought Vicky, as it must have given her so much sorrow to gaze upon it first thing in the morning and last thing at night. Yet perhaps it had also given her a glimmer of hope that one day Walter would see sense?

Linda's bed had not been made since her removal to the hospital three weeks previously, so Vicky now performed this comfortless task.

Leaning over the bed, she kicked a protruding shoe, and there followed a sound of something metal being shifted. On pushing the shoe back in, Vicky saw a small key lying an inch or so from it. She picked it up and examined it. Obviously it was a cupboard key meant to fit a rather flimsy lock. There was but one lock that key fitted; it would be the locker underneath the bedside table. Vicky tried the key in it. It turned easily, and she could not believe her eyes. The locker was filled with documents and letters. Vicky felt a slight guilt about touching them at first, but in the midst of her grief, she realised there would be many others only too eager to assist in the task, if only out of curiosity. Vicky brushed the looser material aside to expose what appeared to be a solid bundle of letters. They were wrapped in a white satin band and a rapid flick through them showed that they all bore German stamps.

She sat on the side of the bed and tried to steady her hand in order to ascertain what they signified. All were addressed to Linda, and all were from Walter, containing pathetic pleadings such as "...I know you will never understand why I did what I did, but please let me come even for one day to see Vicky....I can't wait for the day I will read of your permission to let me see our little girl...I do wish you would not ignore my letters — the past is past...please let me see Vicky..."

Underneath this bundle was another, wrapped in a red satin ribbon. Vicky went once more into shock to discover this bundle comprised ten birthday cards, each containing German bank notes. Although Vicky's feelings at this stage were confused extremes of pain, loss and anger, she settled down gradually into renewed regret that Linda had suffered so much by Walter's leaving. Recalling that day when Linda had explained all to Vicky, she realised that her childish loss, though severe, was but a mild shade of Linda's suffering.

THE bungalow was silent. As morning sunshine bathed Vicky's small bedroom, she shifted her white dressing table slightly so that the mirror would shield her eyes.

Tiredness had taken its exacting toll on those sad eyes. Several used tissues lay crumpled in a tray at her bedside, and she had already changed the pastel cream pillow case, which had become quite damp. There was no sound of her mother's door opening. No gentle rattle as the kettle was filled. No clink of milk bottles being taken in. Vicky's lovely frame once more shook with heaving sobs, and she cursed inwardly the nodding heads that told her, "Life goes on."

"Christ" she said aloud. These people meant well but Vicky was intelligent. How well she knew that "life goes on" equals "I don't know what to say." Suddenly the letter-box clacked as the morning paper tumbled in, followed by two more Mass cards. She couldn't bear to open them, so she deposited them in the black folder supplied by the undertaker. Keys in hand, she walked to her car. It would be her first day back at work after the bereavement. As the new grey 1974 Escort left the driveway, a strange, sad spirit seemed to descend on the empty bungalow. Linda's car, a sturdy little

Wolseley Elf, stood at the shaded gable end, as if in mourning.

The mere routine of slipping through the gears or indicating turns demanded her full concentration. Clearly today was going to be difficult. Vague fears hovered over everything: first morning leaving an empty home, first coffee break, lunch break and so on. Worst of all, the return home after work. As she turned into the Drury Street car park, a lyric from the Fortunes' smash hit droned repeatedly in her brain — "You got your troubles, I've got mine." The pistol-shot banging of car doors in the underground, erratic blasts of horns, and loud, cheery "good mornings" echoing off the concrete walls only reinforced this sentiment.

A short, brisk walk, and the smartly clad Chanel girl had reached Brown Thomas, where it seemed as if life beckoned her to step aboard once more. Indeed her therapy had begun, unknown to her. As she walked to the cosmetic department, the subdued fluorescent lighting extended to her its quiet morning welcome. The richest fragrances seemed to merge with one another at some point in mid-air, and softly descended in gentle benediction, filling every corner.

A kindly hand cupped her elbow, and a gentle voice spoke. "Vicky, if you feel like leaving at lunchtime, it's okay." Vicky thanked the thoughtful cosmetic buyer Mrs Denton, saying she would prefer if she could stick it out until normal finishing time. David Klein, a senior manager, then extended his sympathies. David's six-foot-plus trim frame radiated order and efficiency, but he obviously felt inadequate in matters of bereavement and his attractive shyness certainly did not help matters.

The rest of Vicky's colleagues were just super. Vicky knew there was no need for her to struggle with thoughts or feelings that screamed to find release in words, though any words would be received delicately and discreetly. Some customers also had heard of her mother's death. Several Mass cards were slipped into her hand.

The morning had been quite busy, and lunch hour seemed to come round very soon. Though she was not particularly hungry, it was nice to sit in the restaurant with her two best friends. There the conversation took its own unguided direction, which put Vicky completely at her ease. Sophie from Christine Dior and Louise of the Estée Lauder section were reasonably subdued, given that contagious high-pitched laughter was the more usual hallmark of Sophie's presence. Louise, equally attractive, had an impish little-girl look that disarmed the most threatening superior or customer.

As back to work time drew near, Vicky surprised herself, the trio now alternately huddling and giggling. If the laughter had been raised one decibel, the message, loud and clear, would have been that some devilment was afoot. Though maybe not today!

The afternoon rolled on, the mid-July sunshine glorious in Grafton Street. Yet for those confined to the shop interior, it was becoming bothersome. Obviously the warm dry weather had sent customers to their wardrobes to pull out the lightest, brightest garments they could find. Practically all of the men had donned smart short-sleeved shirts. During a quiet period Vicky filed her thumb nail. Suddenly the penetrating sunshine threw a shadow at her counter. Smiling gracefully, she gave her full attention to the tall, fair-haired man in front of her, who looked to be in his mid-forties. He certainly knew how to dress! The collar of his dazzling white shirt sat on the neck of a smart cream-coloured blazer. A distinctly masculine whiff of some decidedly continental *eau du toilette* wafted about him, belying his American accent. As Vicky wrapped Chanel after-shave balm for him, he handed her a Gold

American Express card. She turned to process the transaction. The name suited him somehow — Dr Hugh Osbourne Burke — as did the card which bore it. As she thanked him, their eyes met once more and Vicky was disturbed. As she commented on the weather, she sensed that those unbelievably deep-set brown eyes had penetrated a great sorrow — some awful trauma. He made a cold, military type bow of the head and went towards the door, where his imposing frame halted. He looked right as if to go in that direction, then suddenly with stately pace he turned towards St Stephen's Green.

"Everything O.K. Vicky?" Sophie had broken Vicky's fast-travelling train of thought.

The voice was gentle, but Vicky was startled and somewhat embarrassed.

"Sure, just day-dreaming," she replied.

In fact, Vicky could still see the expression on that saddened face. The compulsive nature of her musings unnerved her somewhat, as imagination whisked her off to a scene of sad farewell. Had his loved one left him perhaps? Her mind then envisioned a hospital's private consulting room, where he had just told a father of four that six months would be the maximum. Or was he himself informed that he had a dreaded illness? Probably not — he was too fit looking, besides,

Chanel after-shave balm? She then saw him in a chapel praying with silent tears behind a coffin. Perhaps the untimely death of his wife had caused a film of ice to form within the depths of his heart, so that his gaze evoked a scene of Arctic bleakness. In any case, Vicky burned inside to share his thoughts.

COMING home after the first day back at work was dreary. Vicky could not shut out of her head the memories of happier homecomings. Even the gravel driveway seemed especially dusty, and stones crunched under the wheels of the Escort. Melancholy beckoned to her from the abandoned Wolseley nesting close to the side wall. The flowers in the garden looked discontented, needing some tender loving care. Little rain had fallen in the past five weeks. However, other matters called for her attention. Sophie and Louise would arrive in a short while. At present they were in a supermarket assembling the ingredients for a threesome helping of spaghetti Bolognaise. The dining-room needed tidying. Luckily she had remembered to pick up Babycham's favourite cat food, for the little mite always wailed lustily until fed.

Shortly afterwards, the tiny kitten leapt up on the table, amusing Vicky as its white-tipped paw snatched at the crisp wafer-thin pages of a letter she was reading. It was from her dear friend, Brian, in South Africa, and his words of sympathy were helpful. A much-liked member of the squash club to which Vicky also belonged, his previous life as a budding priest had provided him with a wealth of curious and amusing anecdotes.

A Dubliner himself, Brian had inherited a keen eye for horses from his Galway-born father. More than once, a moment of weakness had whisked him off to the Curragh races. Attendance at such meetings was forbidden by his strict Religious order, to which he had belonged for two years. Moreover, the shrewder of the older priests noticed that Brian's aunt's and uncle's sudden illnesses seemed to coincide with major race dates. Yet the charity of their silence wore thin when an RTE camera focussed one afternoon on a certain punter!

Visits to the "houses of seculars", even if only old friends, were also forbidden. One priest, having said night prayers at his bedside, prepared for a night's rest. Suddenly an unheavenly creak greeted his ears. It sounded as if the drainpipe was parting from the wall it had befriended for thirty years, followed by a loud crack and clank. It was the custom for the community to walk the grounds for early meditation, and next morning the tired, unshaven cleric mingled innocently with the devout flock. Suddenly, to his astonishment, his observer of the night before whispered to him:

"Brother, a change of habit would be in order, and mind your back!"

At that Brian hastily checked the hem of his cassock. Thick streaks of mud were layered on that part of the robe that covered the worst bruising. He silently thanked God for Father Gerard's sense of humour, and the matter went no further! Yet general indications were that Brian was not cut out for monastic life, and his departure shortly after did much to restore equanimity among the senior priests.

Not long after leaving the Order, Brian became a very special friend of Vicky's. She had gone out with him a few times, and often wondered why his gestures of affection were so mechanical, when he was obviously such a warm-hearted, handsome-looking chap. Vicky's mother had also been extremely fond of him, and fervently wished that Vicky and he would some day wed. Vicky would never forget a particular night when Brian came in for coffee. She knew for ages that he had had something to say, and indeed had given him every opportunity her intuition afforded. If he were about to ask her to bring their relationship on to a firmer footing, she would not have been displeased. However, his message was not of that order. Rather, he talked to Vicky as if he were revealing a dreaded secret about himself, one that might make her hate him. In short, Brian was gay. In actual fact, however, that night saw the beginning of a most beautiful friendship that would weather the storms of life. Never once did Vicky divulge, even to her mother, Brian's place in the scheme of things. In certain matters the 1970s were very much an unenlightened age!

Entrance into the banking world looked an unlikely career for Brian. However, the world of finance seemed to suit him. He did well, and rapid promotion widened his horizons. Classical music, theatre, financial journals, cinema, combined with the distinct comfort of his own company, made him a content man. The company of women was pleasant to Brian, but not at all compelling. Money, of course, played its part. Then, the previous year, Brian had been offered a managerial posting in South Africa. Saddened to see him go, Vicky was at least happy that he often arranged to ring her for a long chat.

That night Vicky reviewed the day's events. Clearly it had not been as bad as she had expected. Dinner with Louise and Sophie had been particularly enjoyable. Perhaps tomorrow will be even better, she thought, as she turned off the bedside lamp, before whispering a prayer for her mother. Her last drowsy thoughts were of the doctor she had served at the Chanel counter. She smiled at the thought that she felt in any way attracted to the man, who was considerably older, no doubt more than twice her age! But there was something about him, something that intrigued her at this very moment. She had felt such warmth towards him! But then, her own doctor had told her she was still in the grip of her own bereavement. Perhaps that was the answer. Of course, that was it!

VICKY readily grasped the lifelines of work and routine. They, at least, seemed predictable. Happily, today was Tuesday, the weekly "fashion day". Female personnel were to be given a preview of the Christian Dior autumn collection.

For Vicky these fashion days were a weekly injection of magical fantasy. She loved to touch the rich, soft materials, or the fabrics of an attractively rougher quality. It was as if autumn had stepped into the stores and twirled proudly. Shades of brown, gold, russet, red and yellow, were a feast to the eye. Sitting still, the onlooker could in imagination ramble a country lane and view the entire spectrum of October hues. The delicious nutmeg fragrance that wafted through the store suggested the organiser had thought of everything. Galen Weston, the proprietor of Brown Thomas, himself would have been proud. Yet if Vicky imagined it was now autumn, the rising heat of morning told differently!

By coincidence, this was also the day on which French cuisine was promoted. Indeed a glass of wine at mid-morning was unusual. Vicky, Louise and Sophie were already giggling as they took a windowside seat in the Brown Thomas restaurant. Pierre, the chef, looked satisfied, as his merry eye surveyed the *breton quiche, blanquette de veau* and *porc la créme*. Still he was clearly disappointed when the girls explained that they had to return to work. Even topping up their Piat D'Or was out of the question. With a typical French gesture of resignation, he returned the bottle to the shelf. Yet his moustache quivered with delight when they promised they would return at lunchtime.

Their reappearance for the mid-day meal caused Pierre's tall hat to do a little dance. Girlish laughter rose in waves as he helped them to pronounce the names of exotic dishes. He spent quite some time at their table, and once more expressed childish disappointment as they prepared to leave. Clearly he was anxious that they stay and chat, but they had over-stayed their break. Still, any attempt to pay was frustrated by the generous chef who repeatedly insisted, "No — no — it is on the roof!"

Two smartly-dressed executive men dallied in their mutual farewells, thus impeding the girls' progress through the exit. Five long and perfectly manicured fingers belonging to another customer suddenly appeared to hold the door fully back. Vicky was startled as with a slightly awkward shift, he formed a human arch to facilitate the girls. A smart, light blue, cotton jacket replaced the cream-toned blazer he had worn at the Chanel counter. Acknowledging their thanks with a brief "Not at all," he greeted the chef and took his place at one of the now vacant seats. "Nice to see you, Doctor Burke," called Fiona, the smiling waitress, attending to him promptly. Meanwhile, pausing at the door, Sophie and Louise whispered their approval of Dr Hugh's impeccable grooming and instinctive politeness. Yet when they regretted aloud that he was of older vintage, Vicky blushed. A cloud of memory briefly blurred her vision — warm hugs, fatherly concern, petal-light kisses on a little girl's forehead, a feeling of unfailing strength, laughter, security. Yet these were only part of the effect this Dr Burke had upon her, and the ambiguity of his attraction only stirred her imagination. Telling herself the infatuation she felt was nonsense proved useless, however, and she returned to the Chanel counter as if in a day dream.

If not every day bestowed such exotic experiences, working in this main venue of Grafton Street's rapidly pulsing economy meant that excitement was always but a step away. Some months prior to her bereavement, Vicky had served both Michael MacLiammoir and Hilton Edwards. Siobhan McKenna often strolled its many aisles, and Cyril Cusack loved its ambience. A roll-call of its many faithful artistic and literary visitors included Jack B. Yeats, Brendan Behan, and Patrick Kavanagh. Even John Wayne had strode its staircases, and Princess Grace dined there. The Irish eyes of Maureen O'Hara had rested on its chandeliers, and Bing Crosby was known to have loved the store. Indeed its doors had opened to a lengthy queue of well-known Irish and international writers, artists, playwrights, actors and politicians. What's more, a very efficient bush-telegraph system always swung into operation on these occasions, for the Brown Thomas staff was interested to discover what exactly set these people apart from the mainstream of humanity.

The more ordinary day-to-day routine, however, was far from boring. A certain light-hearted strain of good humour had its place and often surfaced in a "when the cat's away, the mice will play" context! On one occasion busy passers-by had been stopped in their tracks by the sight of an all too life-like dummy in the shop window. It was, of course, Sophie, who for a dare, had donned a long blonde wig and posed. Eventually she found it impossible to control her laughter, as curious shoppers passed by and returned to confirm the illusion. On a day preceding an International rugby match, a Scotsman complete with kilt managed the same trick, albeit quaffing a pint of Guinness for good measure. Sophie, caught in the act of leaving her post without permission to see the fellow, quickly explained that she had needed to run after a customer who forgot her change. On another occasion, Zoë, a part-time worker who absolutely adored night-life, collapsed one morning at her counter. A doctor was called who read her racing pulse, and she was ushered to hospital with a suspected heart attack, though those who knew of her frenzied social life were all too aware of the true story behind her symptoms. Ever after, whenever an ambulance-siren sounded in the distance, calls of "Taxi for Zoë" resounded throughout Brown Thomas!

Other similarly secret codes were used to by-pass the ears of certain customers; for example, the approach of a fine specimen of manhood was confirmed by the call MT, for My Type. Likewise, YT meant Your Type, while "There is a mega invoice over there" signified that the girl serving the male customer was fortunate indeed. "Put that back in the drawer; there's a debit note with it", however, signified that the gentleman had a wife or girl friend accompanying him! "No debit note!" indicated the opposite, while "That needs Tipp-Ex," was the coded warning for any extremely unpleasant gentleman.

While some wit had attributed this bizarre behaviour to "cosmetic fall-out," some customs at least had a more serious basis. Traditionally retirement of a girl from the store was occasioned only by marriage. Indeed one particular fairy-tale occasion involved a bus load of American tourists which arrived one afternoon. A particularly helpful girl on the fashion floor greatly impressed one of the party, who asked for her name and promised to call in on her during the following summer. Not only did he, but they fell in love, got married, and went to live in America. After three years of wedded bliss, he died of a heart condition. His wife's grief was overtaken by disbelief, however, when his will revealed him to be a multi-millionaire, the entire inheritance to be hers.

THE alarm-clock woke Vicky from a deep sleep, as unsteady fingers pressed for the stop button on the dancing demon. Her eyes had not deceived her. The laughing clock-face announced that it was definitely 10 o'clock. Apparently adjusting to regular sleeping patterns would be a slow process. She made a phone call, not aware that the same phone call also lessened the anxiety of her Department Manager, who offered a friendly reassurance, and advised her to have some breakfast in the restaurant. Replacing the phone, she made a hurried preparation and set out for work.

Activity in the restaurant was tapering off somewhat. Highly polished round tables reflected the morning sun, while here and there a knife, fork or spoon glistened. A babble of conversation indicated that only a few places were occupied. While she wished the measure of pure orange juice was more generous, the appearance before her of piping-hot scrambled egg on toast was cheering. The rich brown of the butter-melting bread contrasted perfectly with the pale gold resting on it, the aroma tantalizing. Suddenly Vicky was startled by Fiona's voice across the restaurant.

"Beautiful morning, Dr Burke, are you being looked after?"

"Yes indeed, thank you so much."

A second waitress appeared. The breakfast she placed before Dr Hugh three tables away was visibly substantial, though tastefully presented. The eggs, sunny-side-up, still sizzled amidst the surrounding sausages, rashers and tomato. It was difficult to see if that was kidney or liver at the outer side of the large white plate. As he folded *The Irish Times* and laid it neatly within reaching distance, Vicky was mesmerised. She observed every movement: putting his hand into the pocket of the smart beige slacks, taking a pair of lightly tinted glasses and adjusting them slightly on his nose. A playful needle of sunlight flickered on their frame. The slight tint in the lens seemed appropriate, as if the spectacles perhaps helped to contain the haunting, deep-set sorrow of his gaze.

As he alternated between eating, sipping coffee and perusing the nearest section of his morning paper, a steady rhythm became obvious. Occasionally it was necessary to pull the paper to a more convenient angle. Once, rather than turning the page immediately, he laid the neatly-creased pages alongside him for a moment, and then unexpectedly looked left. Vicky almost jumped with embarrassment and averted her inquisitive look with lightning speed. An awkward mixture of fear and desire surged through her. Why did she feel relief when on the margin of her field of vision, she saw him correct the movement with a similar turn to his right? He leaned slightly backward, and continued his triple regimen of eating, drinking and reading. It seemed the first several pages were the limit of his interest, but the breakfast was going down well. Vicky hugged her cup with both hands, and rested her elbows on the table. Peering over the rim of the cup, no one could identify the object of her seemingly idle meandering. Thus she could, in comparative safety, discern that the fawn-coloured short-sleeved shirt bore the Cacharel label; that the light summer slip-ons were of an American style. Navy socks showed when he crossed his legs. Reluctantly she checked her watch and once more turned to leave the aura of this fascinating man. She couldn't help wondering if he would watch her leaving. Or would she see him again? A feeling of tenderness and warmth, mingled with apprehension, once more threw her mind into disarray. Pushing back her chair, her eyes alighted on a volume tucked at the foot of his table. She could just make out the words Freud and Jung along its hard-backed side. Heading towards the exit, she stood back to let Fiona wheel out a tray of plates and saucers. Once outside, she tipped Fiona's wrist and beckoned her into an alcove.

"Just a second," whispered Fiona. Returning with the unloaded vehicle, she stood, hands on the handle, a ready-for-action pose should anyone appear! Nervous bouts of school-girl gigglings then arose spasmodically.

"No, it's worth more than that, Vicky."

"Ok," Vicky responded, her laughter betraying a pleading attitude. "Some fabulous samples of Chanel No 5, then."

Fiona adored good fragrances, but could rarely afford to buy them. "Right then," she continued in a friendly, gossipy vein. "He's an American, but he lives in Howth, drives a Mercedes, loves reading, and he's a psychiatrist."

Vicky's legs were weakening, as Fiona paused.

"Go on, you tease!"

"And he's married with five children."

"Stop messing," cried Vicky.

"Very well," said Fiona. "One more sample next week?"

"All right, all right."

"Well," drawled Fiona, "I'd say he's not married. He has breakfast here most mornings."

"Fiona, you're a pet," beamed Vicky. "Now, breathe a word of this to anyone, and you're dead!"

"Now listen, Vicky, I hope you're not getting any notions. He's old enough to be your father, never mind your analyst!"

Vicky only laughed as she left Fiona to her chores, the laughter more of a nervous release. For her part Fiona had a brief misgiving about breaching a rule of discretion. On second thoughts she decided there was no harm done. Still she resolved never again to give information to any of the girls — at least until her perfume samples ran out!

Back at the Chanel counter, a heightened colour, racing pulse and barely concealed breathlessness were in stark contrast to the Chanel girl's habitually cool, ever-available self.

LIKE Vicky, Sharon had a great zest for life, and this morning clearly some devilment was afoot. Finding it impossible to maintain a dignified pace, the two girls supported each other in a fit of laughter as they emerged from Hickeys where Sharon had helped Vicky select a length of blue material for a dress. While both were highly intelligent girls, their subsequent careful scrutiny of the psychiatry shelves in Hodges Figgis was less than convincing, for this most efficient book shop was a fountain of knowledge for students of all disciplines, and its classification techniques were of the highest order.

The unlikely pair laughed on as they searched for a particular book, working from opposite ends of the shelf. More than once, the nervous replacing of a book caused two or three others to fall. These accidents did not help matters as their composure simply disintegrated. To their horror, the insistingly helpful assistant stood behind them. Obviously a major effort was called for, so Vicky did the talking.

"It's a hard-back, with the words 'Freud and Jung' printed on the spine."

"Is it on any particular book-list for a specific psychiatry course?" the attentive young gent asked.

"Well, not exactly — I mean — I'm not quite sure," replied the fiercely blushing Chanel girl. "It's just that I lost the book — a friend gave it to me, and I'm very anxious to replace it."

"Maybe it's a biographical account of the lives of Freud and Jung?"

"Well, I'm not certain," stammered Vicky, now plainly mortified. Luckily Sharon had had the good sense to move away, for if their eyes had met, the two would have collapsed into mutual hysterics.

"Could you wait there one second?" asked the determined assistant, walking purposefully to another shelf of volumes. Vicky was ecstatic when he returned clutching the very book as if he had made a breakthrough in some highly obscure theory of nuclear physics.

"You see, this is a standard text often used in the psychologist's work. It's a kind of general reference on Jung and Freud. Excellent as a source-book, it deals very well with the major differences of opinion between Freud and Jung, for example on the collective unconscious. I'm sure your friend will be relieved to have it replaced."

Vicky was stuck to the floor. She wished he would just give her the book without wrapping it, and release her from the rapidly soaring discomfort his every word was causing her. If he were to ask for her opinion on the contents of the weighty tome, she felt certain she would die.

Vicky did not have money to throw away, but fifteen pounds was a small price to pay just to get out of the shop. Exactly one step outside the door, and the suppressed skittishness had to be released. Busy shoppers were puzzled by the two pretty girls lying helpless against the window, tears of outrageous laughter streaming down their faces. One girl clutched material for a dress, the other a heavy-looking book, unwrapped!

IT seemed as though everybody had chosen to do their shopping on this Wednesday morning. Perhaps the glorious sunshine lured them out. Several times during the busy morning, Vicky cast an anxious eye on the book she had tucked under the bottom shelf. Each secret peep sent uncontrollable shivers down her spine. Was this a form of madness that possessed her? The moment of truth came when a glance at her watch told her it was eleven o'clock. Decision time. Ignoring the fire of nerves burning in the very centre of her being, she clutched the book and headed towards the restaurant. Happily Louise and Sophie were on a later break, due to the unexpected volume of customers. In the heights of a tizzy, she prayed that her knees would not give way as she passed Fiona.

"Those two seats are reserved," smiled the knowing waitress at Vicky, pointing to the table next to where the Doctor sat. "Certainly," Dr Hugh courteously replied, moving *The Irish Times*, when Vicky asked if it was all right to sit at his table. Her voice, she realised, was not her own, and her hand was unsteady as she placed the book alongside her coffee pot. There was a certain relief in the fact that the newspaper was being constantly adjusted, folded and pressed. Perhaps she could make quick work of this break and get out while the going was good.

Then, unexpectedly, a colleague of hers from the fashion department arrived carrying a white envelope. Embracing Vicky, she explained that news of her mother's death hadn't reached her as she was on holidays. "Vicky, I'm so sorry," her friend comforted her, while Vicky once more re-lived her bereavement and cried.

Alone once more, Vicky tried to compose herself. Still sobbing quietly, she prepared to leave the table. Yet either she was dreaming or was the gentle touch at her elbow for real? Then Dr Hugh spoke, a low-toned, comforting voice suggesting that she might sit for another minute or two. He apologised for intruding on her privacy, explaining that he couldn't help overhearing, and mutual introductions took place. Vicky was lost in embarrassment, yet a strong, affirming hand covered hers.

"Always cry when you feel like it," the calm and steady voice went on. "It is nature's way of dealing with pain."

"Can I ask how many of you are in the family?" he continued after a pause, to which Vicky explained that she was an only child.

"And is your father alive?"

"He left home when I was ten years of age."

Doctor Hugh nodded in sympathy.

"But that was years ago," Vicky added.

"I understand, but with certain children, especially in single-child families, the loss can be a cross they drag to the grave. You may not be aware of it, but when one gets too used to the darkness, one can forget the joy of daylight."

"Losing someone you love cuts to the bone," he added, and Vicky visibly jerked as their eyes met.

"Grieving takes its own course. Intense sadness can lead to anger. We find in ourselves a certain bitterness even towards the one who is gone. We sometimes tell ourselves the death did not occur. We find ourselves in self-torture over what we could have done or something we did do with the best of intentions."

He grew hesitant now, seeming to realise that he was in danger of losing track of his thoughts. Calling for a fresh pot of coffee, he poured a cup for Vicky.

"I see you're studying psychiatry," he said, glancing at the cover of the book. Vicky tried to fight the panic knocking on her heart.

"Not really," she stammered. "I like reading about it, but I'm a beautician — I'm on the Chanel counter here. I actually served you one day."

Obviously he did not remember, but he did remark that Chanel toiletries were his favourite, especially *Pour Monsieur Eau de Toilette*.

Time was moving on, however, and much as she hated doing so, Vicky now made as if to leave. Once more Dr Hugh's hand covered hers.

"Don't forget, Vicky, there will be good days and bad days, but the good days will come more often than you now think."

Dr Hugh remained standing until she had left the restaurant. Next to him, the two "reserved" seats were still unoccupied, testifying to the success of Fiona's clever scheme!

SEVERAL days later Vicky witnessed a sheer graciousness shine forth from the old lady's wrinkled face, whose trip to the Chanel counter had clearly been rewarded. Her little hands cupped a dainty handkerchief on which Vicky was spraying a fragrance for her. Smiling, she declared, "Ah, there was a time when I could make heads turn, my dear, for I was once beautiful too."

Her eyes twinkled and Vicky could have hugged her. Yet unknown to Vicky, Dr Hugh was observing the touching scene. He waited as the lady shuffled away, then approached the surprised Vicky, who had just glanced at her watch.

"I hope you don't mind — I just thought I'd call in to see how you are."

"Oh — I'm fine, thank you...That was really kind of you," replied Vicky, who was plainly thrilled to see him. There followed an awkward pause, broken by their two voices uttering something at the same moment. It seemed both had intended going for a coffee!

Once in the Brown Thomas restaurant, Dr Hugh pulled back a chair for Vicky. When both were seated face to face, Fiona appeared behind Dr Hugh. If Vicky was already excited, Fiona's winking certainly did not help matters. Dr Hugh, however, had the knack of making one feel at home, and in no time Vicky was deep in conversation with him. Savouring his calm, manly presence, she felt a great sense of safety in his company.

He appeared delighted that she played squash, and that her reappearance at the club was further helping to bring her once more into the mainstream of life. Vicky explained that the other members were friendly, but was careful to emphasise the fitness aspect, and the warm, but platonic, nature of her attachments there. Dr Hugh explained to her that her sleeping pattern would return to normal in time, and that exercise would help. Unconsciously lapsing into tingly laughter, Vicky found herself telling him about Babycham, her black and white kitten.

"The little monkey has me wrapped around her little finger — she has no manners, and has the run of the house. She goes with the speed of lightning, and I can't even turn the page of a book without her wanting to play with it."

Dr Hugh laughed, then suddenly assumed a more serious air. "How are you getting on with the book, Vicky? You know, the one on Freud and Jung?"

Vicky's heart missed a beat, several beats. It was as if a slight tremor had shaken Grafton Street, and she could feel the blood draining from her face.

"Well, it's a bit complicated," she stammered. "But quite interesting."

In the deafening silence, Vicky wished she had never cooked up the "book" scheme. She made a rapid search in every nook and cranny of her agile mind to find a change of subject, but it was hopeless.

"Would you agree that Jung was bound in conscience to go his own way?" Dr Hugh prompted. Desperate, Vicky remembered something from her harrowing conversation with the assistant in the bookshop, and grasped at it urgently.

"Everyone, I suppose, has to do what they think is right. It was over the collective unconscious, wasn't it?"

"Indeed," mused Dr Hugh.

Having pretended to check the time, a life-saving tactic in moments like this, Vicky was not quick enough to capture a rapid, kindly smile transform the psychiatrist's face. Thankfully he changed the subject, and Vicky could breathe again.

"I suppose, what with all your squash-club activities and your friends at the club, you don't have much time to spare?" Dr Hugh then asked.

"Well, I do keep some time for myself — just to do my own things."

"Good! It's important to have your own personal time."

Vicky's heartbeat gathered momentum.

"I was wondering, that is, if you had an evening to spare — perhaps we could go for a meal?" said Dr Hugh. Once more Vicky thought she was dreaming, only this was a truly wondrous dream! "Why, I'd love to Dr Hugh," she heard herself reply.

"Please call me, Hugh," he said, the words travelling past her. "What side of town do you live on, Vicky?"

Awakening, she told him she lived on the south side.

"Right," he replied. "I know a really nice restaurant in the Dublin mountains, called Killakee House."

Vicky knew where it was, but had never dined there.

"Would Friday at, let's say, 8.30 be O.K.?" he asked.

A delighted Vicky said that would be perfect, as he took careful note of her address. Fiona almost toppled over her trolley on seeing Dr Hugh and Vicky leave together. Dr Hugh bade farewell to Vicky at the Chanel counter. As he walked out, he called back to Vicky as if in afterthought, "And we must have a good chat about Freud and Jung."

Fortunately the full impact of that remark did not immediately hit Vicky, who was in another world, yet still aware that Dr Hugh walked out of Brown Thomas on this occasion with a somewhat lighter step.

Once he was out of sight, Louise found an immediate excuse to visit Vicky's counter. There was a hubbub, and Sophie swiftly joined the two excited girls. Once more, the best of their efforts could not suppress gasps of amazement and occasional cries of excitement. Zoë's voice was heard nearby, remarking, "Well isn't it great to see Vicky coming back to herself!"

Suddenly there fell an unexpected hush on the trio, as Vicky grew totally perplexed, utterly puzzling Louise and Sophie.

"I'm in dire straits," she cried. "The book — the damn book!"

Tears of laughter mingled with nervous stammers and gasps, as she explained how she had used the book in her efforts to attract the attention of Dr Hugh, and how the whole plan had backfired. Any trace of dignity deserted Louise and Sophie, who were already sick with laughter. Reality was rapidly closing in on Vicky, and speech failed her. Her blue eyes made a silent, pleading appeal to her two friends. When the girlish skittering came to a halt, she explained urgently that a brief look through the book had yielded no understanding whatsoever. At that point Louise jumped to the rescue. She was an avid reader, and promised Vicky that she would comb it for the most important points, and explain it piecemeal to Vicky as a bird feeds its young. Vicky gave her the book from where she had hidden it, and the storm-clouds seemed to lift.

Hoping to negotiate this obstacle, Vicky's mind slid back to her days in secondary school, where she had been an expert at scheming. Suddenly there appeared in her mind's eye the stern countenance of Sister Joseph as she once again admonished a repentant Vicky.

"You'll always fall into your own trap — a liar must have an excellent memory, Vicky." Indeed there had always been the occasional scheme that failed. Would this current plan prove one of them? Perish the thought!

The following morning Louise arrived breathless. She was a poor time-keeper all right, but this morning being five minutes late was not the only cause of her agitation.

"Vicky — I just can't get a handle on it — it's bloody double dutch. I was going at it hammer and tongs all last night — and until two o'clock this morning. I'll need two bloody matchsticks to keep my eyes open today. It must be a specialists' psychiatry book, and you'd need a dictionary to help you chop through it — uggh !! I'm really sorry."

Regretfully, she slipped the book back to Vicky, who was stunned. Sophie then came over to the Chanel counter as if she had serious business there. It wouldn't do for the three tear-aways to be seen huddling together, so she pretended to be looking for something from the higher shelves, talking at the same time. Louise gave her the gist of the goings-on, and the inevitable happened, all three succumbing to uncontrollable guffaws.

"You'll have to come clean," said the slowly recovering Sophie.

"Look — if I've to eat the blessed thing for a week, I'll do it. I couldn't let him know. I'd just die a thousand deaths," cried Vicky.

All three once more fell into fits of laughter. The store manager became alarmed, and a sprightly walk brought him into view of the startled trio. With an almighty effort, they straightened up as if they had been discussing business and were about to return to their duties immediately, which they did. Alone again, Vicky looked at the book near her foot, and wondered if this was what a panic attack must be like. What's more, Sophie's last remark raced through her mind.

"If he's a psychiatrist, Vicky, he'll know every little trick you get up to."

Jung and Freud dominated Vicky's life for several days after. Even Babycham was somewhat set to one side. It was tortuous to spend evening after evening wading through the stuff, none of which made sense to her otherwise bright mind. Determined not to give in, she struggled desperately with the undigestible material, yet it was futile. Just when she thought she was winning, a tiny sentence at the end of a paragraph would prove her grasp of the subject to be sheer imagination. Hours of hard slogging did not help her recall any of it, and the words of Sister Joseph haunted her.

"Don't jump into the water, girl, if you cannot swim."

Already over her head, she decided against all odds to keep swimming. She never was a quitter, anyway. But what a price to pay!

JULY had kept its promise of fine dry weather and daily sunshine. Friday morning dawned tranquilly, broken only by the occasional shutter being raised for commencement of a busy day. Grafton Street itself was a sleepy wonderland, as it made a grudging effort to awaken fully and receive the already increasing heat. Vicky walked along it with a light step, thinking of the dress she would wear that evening. Sharon was a genius, and Dr Hugh would think it cut from the blue sky. Every inch of it from neck to knee flattered her attractive figure. It was good to be alive!

The steady trickle of customers did not prevent an exchange of laughter and innuendo between Vicky, Louise and Sophie. Their counters were only a few feet apart, an arrangement the store manager often regretted. While he did not lack a sense of humour, he certainly embodied discipline and efficiency himself. Vicky shortly heard the distant creaking of his highly-polished shoes. Soon he was at her side, gliding his thumb up and down the clip of his fountain pen, a sure sign of things not being, as he would put it, "altogether correct." Indeed it was said of him that he could hear the grass growing, and he needed no particular insight to know that something very peculiar had been stirring during the past few days. As such, Vicky breathed a sigh of relief when he finally disappeared.

The brilliant sunshine had turned St Stephen's Green into a tropical holiday resort, the blossoms on the trees in full bloom. Vicky had found a quiet seat where the sun did not beat down directly. It was, she thought, the perfect place for today's lunchtime. An elderly gentleman, obviously retired, sat reading his newspaper on the far end of the bench. Voices of excited children and the constant quacking of ducks were a pleasant distraction, yet Vicky was agitated. If the book in her hand was still brand new, it had acquired a look of having been read and re-read. Running her palm over a page, she winced at the heat, realizing she must have fallen asleep with the book open. A book that was now the bane of her life, an instrument of physical and psychological torture, physical because it caused her deprivation of sleep, and psychological because its contents were always just beyond her reach. She snapped it closed in frustration, the receipt she used as a bookmark rising into the air and landing on the grass a few feet away. When the kindly gentleman at her side retrieved it for her, she thanked him and smiled, saying a silent prayer that he would not start a conversation with her. Just as her plea sailed heavenward, fate decided otherwise. Certainly an older Dublin man was not going to ignore another sharing a seat with him, especially if the occupant was young and lovely!

Still Vicky remained polite as he talked of the weather, the cost of living, Ireland going into the EEC, the growing problem of vandalism and what he would do with the culprits! Eventually Vicky's patience wore thin, especially after several obvious efforts to re-start her reading did nothing to put him off. She tried to resign herself, having discovered in her daily work that conversations with older folk had a sort of pattern about them. And this chat was no exception, she realised; what's more, he must be coming to a close, as she heard him invite her to guess what age he was. She tried not to be over-generous, as that would take the good out of it. She put him at about ten years on the fair side of seventy-five, then managed to look amazed when he announced his age of seventy-one in the manner of a court witness speaking under oath. She was confident he was ready to go when he replaced his newspaper in his pocket and lifted his walking stick which hung on the back of the seat, but then suddenly his eyes rivetted onto the cover of her book, stretching her nerves to the breaking point.

"Ye know, love, you're very young to be reading books like that. Ye see, these mind-readers — like that Freud fella — and whatcha call 'im — they're only trying to get control of yer mind — then they can do anythin' they want. Ye see — that's how yer man Freud used to go on — beggin' your pardon, Miss, with all that quare talk about the facts of life thing — ye know love ? Pagans they all were — not an ounce of religion in any of them. If I was you, I wouldn't give them the satisfaction of reading any of their books — I'd buy detective stories..."

"Jesus," Vicky prayed, "please make him leave now!" Seeming to read her mind, the old fellow hobbled off towards the lake.

Alone on the bench, Vicky didn't know whether to laugh or cry. She closed her eyes and tried to concentrate. If Dr Hugh asks me about the book what options have I? I can just say I read it briefly, or I can say I read certain sections of it. Perhaps I can throw back the question to him and agree with his reply all the way. Now that's a clever one — why didn't I think of that before — but hold on! He's a psychiatrist — he'd cop on. "Bloody Hell!" cursed Vicky, who rarely swore, even silently! She had visions of informing him she had a migraine, nor would she have any trouble manufacturing one with this level of stress. Still, it was not a totally unpleasant torment, rather of the pleasure-pain variety!

VICKY'S bedroom had stored up the day's heat and brightness. She leaned forward towards the dressing-table mirror, and removed a tiny speck of powder from her eye-lash. A delightful sub-plot, she saw, was taking place behind her, where Babycham sat on a bookshelf, an adorable kitten with truly funny markings. In the dark the white tips of her paws and the sheer white of her chest were just visible. She watched intently as Vicky prepared for her date, turning her head in tune with Vicky's every movement, the little eyes full of wonder. If only she could speak, she would ask a thousand questions! Vicky's face broke into a splendid smile at the thought, and she longed to lift the little creature and play with it, but that would undo a lot of preparation.

Instead she again regarded herself in a silence broken only by the whisper of a string of pearls that she fingered lovingly on both sides of her neck. Once again she tried to imagine how her mother had felt as Walter, Vicky's father, told his wife to go ahead and open the red velvet box that had contained them. Suddenly these thoughts threatened to pull her down. If only she could pose and twirl for the delighted eyes of her dear mother. What she would give just to have Linda's words of praise and wishes of "Good luck, darling." Tears welled up within her as she reflected on her mother's death. A terrible blow, yet it was that very event which through many twists and turns had led her to this glorious evening.

The crunching sound of tyres on gravel suddenly set her heart beating fast. With great self-restraint she refused to dash to the window. However, Babycham scurried for cover as the doorbell summoned Vicky from her stool, pulling her headlong in a mad dash towards the hall. She straightened her dress before opening the door with a super-human effort to look composed. A stately, gently smiling Dr Hugh took her hand and laid a feather-light kiss on her cheek. Before she could ask him in, he disengaged her hand and stood back. Words were unnecessary, as he bathed her from head to toe with those deep, deep eyes. A slow side-to-side shake of his head and the accompanying release of a deep breath was his eloquent compliment. Vicky thrilled at his silent language. Not a hint of crude passion, simply a manly appreciation that went far beyond the silly phrases of younger men. Yet his candid, studied gaze made her feel all woman.

Declining the offer of a drink, Vicky noticed that he was studying a portrait in the sitting room. A beautiful ballerina stood poised in its golden frame. Linda was well-known in the world of pirouette and pom-pom. Having heard the significance of the charming painting, Dr Hugh seemed a little slow to shift his attention to the framed photo of Vicky's father on the cabinet. He made a discreet remark about how photography had changed over the years, and Vicky was relieved that he had so tactfully indicated the limit of his interest. She herself firmly put aside any thought of letters that never kindled a response, of cards that never got to speak their greeting. No evil thought from that cauldron of gloom was going to bubble up and cast a nasty air over this happy, happy evening.

The narrow roads to Killakee House provided the perfect setting for a wonderful evening. Unkempt bushes on either side looked on in approval as the Mercedes easily took the twists and turns. Here and there, stolen patches of forest floor revealed tiny wayside flowers still smiling in their evening shade. As every upwards bend rewarded the two travellers with a wider view all round, their conversation receded. Instead Hugh and Vicky shared a single invisible partner — togetherness.

At Killakee, an old courtyard served the restaurant as car-park. Two hundred and fifty years of clanging hooves and trundling cartwheels had resounded in that rectangle. A large bell-tower rose from one corner. In former days it summoned the mountainy labourers to their tasks in the morning and likewise sounded the end of their toil in the evening. A lantern still mounted on two outstretched iron arms once threw its light on the scene. While Vicky had never been here before, Hugh was clearly pleased that she was so observant.

They spent almost five minutes taking in the sheer wonder and old-worldliness of the scene. Hugh's heart stood still, as Vicky stooped down and picked a tiny, blue forget-me-not, a chance child of nature that peeped out from a crack in the slab at the entrance to the restaurant, itself foot-worn and weather-beaten. Totally unself-conscious, she gazed at it, then put it to her nose. No word was spoken, yet an eternal moment was born, a moment that Hugh locked in the recesses of his heart, before throwing away the key.

THE Killakee House Restaurant was not purpose built, which enhanced its charm. The day's light was waning and so the delicate interior light was more in evidence. A large kitchen dresser stood at one wall, a display-case for the blue-rimmed plates, cups and cosy tea-pot which were relics of older times. Candle-light threw shadows on the rafters, giving the delph a life of its own.

The meal was excellent. Hugh had been most attentive in a quiet, unobtrusive way. Coffee was now served, and deeper conversation seemed imminent, as the night was young. Vicky stated that she loved working in Brown Thomas. She shared with Hugh the light and serious side of life in the cosmetic world. As she spoke, it was clear that he had entered her world, and moved about in it with her. Her blue eyes danced as she spoke, and her tinkling laughter was a joy to his ears. The ebb and flow of conversation lulled then for a short while. Two more cups of coffee arrived. Hugh assumed a serious but kindly expression, which Vicky took as a signal that he had drawn various strands of thought together and was ready to take a lead. Silently, she cried to God for help, "Please God — don't spoil a terrific evening — make him forget the book!" Meanwhile Hugh looked intently at her, resting his elbows on the table, and placing the tips of his fingers together so that his chin rested on the arch. She tensed, certain now that questions about the book would roll out, as his pose suggested a more serious turn of mind. Watching the candle lantern casting magical shades on his bronze-tanned face, she almost missed him remark,

"As I've learned so much about you, a little information about myself would now be in order. Anyhow, I live in Howth, Vicky, having moved to Ireland fifteen years ago. My psychiatric practice enabled me to buy a property here. Well, truth to tell, my wife's psychologist's income at the time also came into the reckoning."

The radiating flickers on Vicky's fair complexion challenged his concentration, and he paused, idly rearranging the pink napkin. Before she could speak, he once more cast a restrained glance at her, then feeling uncomfortable, avoided her gaze for a moment. Thunderstruck, Vicky instantly recalled the pain she sensed in the windows of his very soul when he first appeared at the Chanel counter. She felt embarrassed as he swallowed hard, obviously exerting the utmost self-control to continue.

"We had a little boy — Karl, whom we idolised. For his eighth Christmas he wanted a bike. Barbara insisted that it would be a foolish gift for a lively young chap flying around Howth Head, who would inevitably want to be going to school on it. I thought she was over-reacting, and presented the hidden gift to him on Christmas morning. Late in February a Garda Squad arrived at our home, where we heard the horrific story of his death. In fact Barbara was advised not to come to a formal identification."

There was a lengthy pause as once more he cupped a wine glass, turning it in his palms. Clearing his throat, he spoke again,

"I loved my wife, Vicky , but after that horrendous loss, a terrible emptiness invaded our lives. We could not communicate and slowly drifted apart. Eventually we separated. She is now back in America. Sounds crazy, but that's how it is. I was thinking of leaving Howth — the house is full of memories."

A sudden look at Vicky and he thought of two blue saucers being filled with water.

"Vicky — please forgive me — how selfish — and you still in bereavement. Come — let's finish that wine."

He placed his hand on hers. To his delight, she reached over and placed her other hand on top of his. The candle-lantern played on two smiling faces, and the waiter refilled their empty glasses.

As the Mercedes whirred smoothly along the narrow mountain road, Hugh rejoiced in Vicky's gasp of delight. The view was spectacular, and he was only too pleased to park the car in a lay-by, where both got out of one accord. The thousands of shining city lights below lay like tapered candles in the still night air, their flames pointing steadily to Heaven as if in praise.

"That's Howth Head way over there," Hugh finally spoke in his quiet voice with its pleasant American flavour. Vicky immediately picked out the distant shape, a mighty hump that resembled the back of a dinosaur, its head dipping into the black sea. A distant track of orange-coloured streets lights highlighted its spine. Two lighthouses, one in deeper water, beamed at intervals. Vicky did not hear Hugh return to the car, and was conscious only of two sensitive hands pressing a gaberdine on her shoulders.

"You know, Vicky, this is a very dangerous area at this time of morning!" he said, his face taking on a school-boy, rascal-like expression. "A huge black cat roams about these hills in the darkness.

You remember the painting in the restaurant? It's supposed to be the devil."

Vicky chuckled and nestled close to him. This time of year, darkness visited but briefly. The night sky was determined to make the best of it, and the moon threw a wide sheet of light over the scene. Twinkling stars kept their silent watch. Hugh and Vicky sat on a low stone wall. She said she didn't mind if he smoked, loving the way the match lit up his face. A few long draws and the rich aroma from his pipe enveloped them. He told her it was Erinmore, his favourite Irish tobacco. Vicky drew the gaberdine a little tighter over her shoulders. "Hugh," she said, then stopped as if the words would not come. Finally she managed to speak her mind.

"I've a confession to make."

Hugh's heart sank as a heavy stone would to the ocean floor, though he felt he should be thankful for at least this one night of bliss. As she went on, however, his spirits suddenly soared again, on powerful wings.

"That book — I feel so ashamed." Vicky was looking away from him.

"I only used it as a trick to catch your attention. Please forgive me. I know absolutely nothing about psychiatry. Hugh, I confess I intended to lie to you..."

Though Hugh was turning her head back towards him, she found it hard to look straight at him. Suddenly he stood, and his pipe fell sideways, spilling its redness onto the grass. A tremendous laugh rang out, and Vicky was dismayed. Finally he sat down and frantically wiped the tears from his eyes. She was astounded as he placed his hands on the back of her neck, as if he were about to kiss her passionately.

"Vicky, Vicky, Vicky," he cried, joy and laughter surging through him. "You wicked, wicked minx!"

"Can I tell you something, Vicky?" he continued after a deep breath. "I fell in love with you the minute you shied away from my remarks about psychiatry. You remember — in the restaurant. I knew then you were not exactly into the shenanigans of Freud and Jung!"

Vicky was overjoyed, as Hugh released her and composed himself further. It was useless, however, for his laughter erupted again. Finally he settled down, and hands on his lap, spoke seriously.

"Vicky I have a confession to make. I tried like hell to find out about Chanel cosmetics — or any cosmetics for that matter. I know nobody in that line, and only for that I would have bewildered you with my extensive knowledge."

This time the hills rang with spontaneous laughter from them both.

Eventually, silence reigned one more, only to be broken by Hugh's soft-spoken words.

"Vicky, truth to tell, I get enough of psychiatry." He looked at the ground and tapped his retrieved pipe. "I don't quite know how to say this — but you have done more for me tonight than Freud and Jung could do together. Thank you, thank you, Vicky."

From above the moon looked down on a tender scene. Hugh re-arranged the gaberdine on Vicky's shoulders to fend off the now chilling air. He could not resist drawing her to him in a gentle, chaste embrace, and Vicky wished time would stand still, she felt so utterly safe in his arms.

The return journey was all too short. As Hugh walked her to her door, Vicky tingled with anticipation.

"Vicky, would you please come out with me again?"

"Give me your diary," she smiled. Dumb-founded, he did so, and watched with amazement as she placed a tiny blue flower in its centre before closing the diary and handing it back to Hugh. The little flower she had picked at the entrance to the restaurant.

"I'd love to, Hugh — I'd love to."

MONDAY mornings were never like this. No doubt the prolonged sunshine drew forth a well of general kindness and goodwill, but Vicky's zest for life and overall high spirits arose from a different source! Indeed her feet hardly touched the pavement of Grafton Street as she headed for work.

At Brown Thomas, Mr Klein, the store manager, was still in shock. Galen Weston, the proprietor of the store, was due to make one of his official visits in the afternoon. It was essential that every detail be in order. Mr Klein was examining a slight stain on the carpet at close range. As he arose, a flying missile from the direction of the stairway caught the side of his head, a solid blow, heavy enough to knock him off balance. For a second or two he even thought he had suffered a minor stroke. Indeed he had been struck, but with a most unlikely object. The dust cover of a hard-back volume had fallen directly at his feet, and the book itself lay downwards. Along its spine his dazed eyes could just make out the words Freud and Jung!

Vicky stood on the stairway absolutely appalled. How was she to know that Mr Klein's head would surface from behind a counter at the exact moment that she would toss the book away in a burst of joy? She stood in his office like a repentant schoolgirl. It was best to say nothing and just accept the dressing down. Mr Klein was furious, and quite sore, his dignity shattered. Yet Vicky was genuinely sorry, and disarmed by her large appealing eyes, Mr Klein found that he could not vent his fury fully on her, as she assured him that it had been only carelessness on her part, a total accident. And so he accepted her convincing apology.

Still the incident had told him it was not going to be a good day. What's more, his fear was fed by the constant huddlings and giggles of the troublesome trio! Every time he disappeared, the urgent whispers of Vicky, Louise and Sophie gathered momentum, all too often spiralling into an uproar. He sensed, however, that neither he, nor his mishap, was the centre of their attention. Rather something had been driving those girls giddy for several days past, some other strange catalyst was at work, something more than just the warm weather.

His misgivings were further confirmed around mid-day, when Mr Klein normally spent from eleven to twelve o'clock in his office. Since the day was extremely hot, Sophie was unanimously chosen to sneak out and buy ice-cream cones for the girls on cosmetics, ten cones in all! Such delinquencies were not unknown! To be doubly sure that everything was "under control", Sophie was to knock on the window three times and the girl at the counter nearest the window would give the all-clear. Meanwhile the ever-inventive Sophie made ten holes in the top of a cardboard box in order to carry the cones. The blazing sun was already wreaking havoc on the ice cream as she stood knocking on the window of Brown Thomas. No returning signal! Knock, knock, knock! No signal back. Several more hard knocks, as two Gardai walked by, looked quizzically, and went on. They then turned and stopped and stared, one of them grinning at Sophie, who was mortified. She peered through the window from every angle, but could see no reason why the agreed signal had not been returned. Frustrated and absolutely embarrassed, she walked in as a customer held the door for her. Directly inside stood a disbelieving and furious Mr Klein, staring at the melted ice cream floating about the box held in Sophie's trembling hands.

Shortly after Galen Weston came as promised. Every girl, including the "terrible trio", played their part and Mr Klein relaxed once more. The cosmetic girls raved about Galen Weston, struck by his tall, athletic figure. Whispered admiration spread like wildfire as he strolled about chatting here and there. Yet Vicky's remarks were quite restrained, tellingly so, as her heart was already given to a man more than twenty years older than herself. Indeed she could not wrench her thoughts from the prospect of meeting Hugh tomorrow. Then, for the first time, she would cross the threshold of Seagrave House.

SEAGRAVE House was surely master of all it surveyed. It faced the sea, so that a fine marine vista stretched both left and right. It looked more like the home of a retired sea-captain then that of a psychiatrist. The wrought-iron gate sported a cabin wheel, and two glass net weights adorned the pillars. Clusters of dazzling white and sky-blue border flowers skirted the tightly-trimmed lawns. Pleasant lapping of water sounded from a two-tiered circular fountain in the centre. Once inside, the layout of the large hall declared that Hugh had a keen eye for antiques. A long gold-framed mirror stood guard over a large mahogany table, itself a masterpiece of loving craftsmanship. Long hours of detailed chiselling had left an intricate pattern of leaves and branches in its wake, and Hugh could see Vicky regarding it in awe.

It subsequently transpired that Hugh was also an excellent cook, though Vicky laughed when he donned a neat white apron. He insisted that she have a glass of his favourite wine as an aperitif. As she sat, he chatted from the adjoining kitchen. Sipping the wine, she realised that there were many sides to this amazing man. A collection of hundreds of classical music LPs lined several shelves along with many books of Irish interest. She guessed that the largest of these contained photographic material. Vicky also thrilled to see the piano by the window. Obviously he had been playing it recently, as its keyboard was visible and sheet music rested on the stand. Vicky's attention was subsequently gripped by the brightly coloured painting on the wall opposite her. Four sprightly white horses dashed riderless along a strand. It was so vivid, she nearly had to duck to avoid a flying hoof. Her wondering eyes then once more surveyed the very real expanse of sea that surrounded Howth Head, where sail-boats skimmed the water in the distance.

Totally engrossed, she was startled by a call in a mock-French accent. "Dinner ees served, Madame."

Hugh appeared at the door with the white apron draped over his left arm. With a half-bow and sweeping flourish of his right hand, he indicated that Vicky might enter. With a theatrical gesture he offered her his arm and escorted her towards the dining room, his impersonation of the haughty host just right, and his light-hearted approach putting Vicky very much at ease.

On entering the dining room, Vicky stopped in her tracks. Hugh thrilled as she gazed at the setting, taking in a vision of exquisite beauty. She stared at the table covered with elegant Irish linen, in its centre a vase of roses, their petals translucent with sunlight that seemed to suffuse the entire room, highlighting the white delph that bore hand-painted floral motifs. Silverware claimed its share of gleaming sunlight as did the Waterford crystal which threw prism-like darts at various angles. As she took it all in, Hugh heard her gasp, "It's only magnificent!"

On a sideboard nearby stood two trophies. A discreet closer look informed Vicky they were for running, and she could just make out the name "Karl" on both. Above the sideboard hung an oil-painting of a dark-haired woman. Her high cheek bones were accentuated by dark shades which blended into sensuous, but still somewhat severe, lips. Turning away, Vicky tried to take in the breath-taking reality that she was to spend this evening with Hugh. While life throbbed in the almost tropical weather outside, here Hugh and Vicky could, for a little time at least, live in a world of their own, accompanied only by the subdued strains of Chopin which seemed to reassure her.

And what a meal it was! Vicky had only a moderate appetite, but Hugh's way with French cuisine took care of that. The entire meal lasted two hours, and throughout Hugh guided proceedings expertly. Vicky noticed that he had a clever knack of mingling light conversation with moments of meaningful silence. Yet she felt that if she wanted to speak of a serious matter, he could offer her his full attention. And could he tell a funny story!

Were Vicky to thank Hugh for the wonderful meal as profusely as her inner heart urged, she knew she would make a fool of herself. The meal, after all, was secondary. The important thing was the precious togetherness which meant everything. Still she thought it would be polite at least to indicate that it might be time to leave, in case Hugh had duties to attend to. For his part, Hugh flustered within — should Vicky get the impression that he would be in any way possessive after such a short acquaintance. Killakee House had been beyond his wildest dreams, and this evening's meal seemed a hundred percent success.

And so a lull in the conversation accommodated both their preoccupations; then as happened on the morning they first went for coffee, they both spoke simultaneously. Undoubtedly a brief mental telepathy had occurred, and laughing, each gave way to the other. Hugh ventured first, "Vicky, the evening is young. I'd be so pleased if you could stay a while." Vicky's delight barely allowed her to utter, "Of course — I'd love to!"

They were now standing, and Hugh took her hand and squeezed it, as they adjourned to the parlour. Without warning, Hugh plonked himself down on the piano-stool. He made as if to spread the tails of an imaginary dress-suit coat over the back of the stool. His fingers then rippled along the ivories in nonsensical fashion, rapidly covering the entire keyboard as he crossed hands in an almost impossible fashion. Vicky was helpless with laughter, his unpredictable prankishness once more endearing him to her.

When he ceased, however, Vicky could no longer refrain from remarking on the two photos on the piano top. In response, a saddened Hugh explained what Vicky had already surmised. The beautiful woman was the same woman portrayed in the oil-painting hanging over the side-board in the dining room. The other of course was of eight-year-old Karl, an informal posy of flowers lying in front of it.

"Your wife is very beautiful," Vicky finally stammered. Hugh was silent for a few moments, before answering. "Yes, Vicky, but beauty is never quite enough. Without love, what is there?" He gazed vacantly at the piano top, then sighed, "Can anything exist without love?"

Turning back to Vicky he continued. "The ebbing tide of life has stolen my happiness, but its return has brought me a precious treasure, you, Vicky. You have brought light into darkness, brought love into my life."

He stopped as if he regretted speaking, but Vicky's gentle embrace told him everything was perfect and he smiled once more. He re-seated himself on the piano stool, then standing up, made a mock bow and announced in an equally mock German accent, "Zis is Fur madam Victoria," at which Vicky giggled and curtsied.

Vicky was impressed by the fact that while Hugh's frivolous send-up of a concert pianist belied the fact that he was a skilful pianist, he himself seemed totally unconscious of it. Moreover, every chord Hugh struck on the piano wrenched at her heart. He was playing *Für Elise*, and the tune pulled her into a sudden melancholy. At first she thought of the flowers at the young boy's photo, but no — it wasn't that. Suddenly she thought of her front parlour at home. She saw the piano still there, unplayed for years. It then came to her that her father had played that very tune, thousands of times it seemed. After his mysterious disappearance she had never liked hearing it. Come to think of it, her mother had never opened that piano since he left, and Vicky herself had stopped going to music lessons. So, all in all, listening to Hugh's playing was truly a bitter-sweet affair, yet she made a gallant effort to smile and applaud.

Outside dusk was descending, indicating how much time had passed.Still seated on the piano-stool, Hugh admired Vicky's youthful figure outlined against the bay-window. Turning, she walked over to him, put her arms around him and gently kissed him. "Hugh, you know this is like one great love-story — just like the story I would love to write some day." And the Mercedes that glided its way back to her bungalow shortly after carried the two main characters of that very tale.

IN the weeks that followed, Vicky soon learned that Howth had everything to offer. There was the constant round of restaurants, including several cosy bistros in the vicinity. The Abbey Tavern also offered a superb night's entertainment. Strangely it was the severe aspect of its stone walls and wooden tables that enhanced the atmosphere once the ballad group struck up. These nights brought out an irresistible boyish attractiveness in Hugh. He was not entirely familiar with traditional Irish music, but Vicky often noted how, during a particularly rousing tune, he would look round with an air of satisfaction at the stamping crowd. Suddenly the mood of the session would change and a slow rendering of an old love song would lull the audience. On several occasions Hugh asked her the story behind a particular ballad. If she did not really know, a devilment in her compelled her to concoct one. More often than not, he saw through the fraud, and revelled in the impish plot. His favourite song was *Carrickfergus*, which told the story of how two lovers became separated, yet the love-smitten man tells how, "I would swim over the deepest ocean my love to find." Needless to say, Hugh was overjoyed when Vicky soon gave him a LP that included it.

Since Vicky hadn't gone horse-riding for many years, Hugh was apprehensive when she mentioned her love of horses. He need not have worried. Observing her slipping a rein smoothly through her fingers while drawing the horse's head round with the other confirmed that she was re-acquiring the knack rapidly. Hugh's heart beat fast when she slid into an easy trot, that tightened into a canter before she sat into a thundering gallop. He relaxed as he sat on his own mount, taking in the glorious scene, relieved that her love of horses was matched by considerable skill.

For her part, Vicky was nervous at first on stepping into Hugh's boat, the *Sea Scamp*. The creaking in the timbers of the small craft was new to her, as was the entire sensation of the whipping sails as the bow cut a furrow through the rolling waves. Hugh realised she was unsure at first, but was pleasantly surprised when she told him she wanted to learn the art of sailing. He was an expert teacher, and they had many hours of fun on the sea. Eventually Vicky became quite adept. On one particularly hot day when the wind refused to oblige, Vicky looked with wonder as his bronze arms and sinewy shoulders moved in time to the oars for twenty minutes, Hugh humming

Carrickfergus all the time! Sometimes he would deliberately let an oar slip and pretend he did not notice. Then, a frantic leap into the water to recover it while she tried to hang on to the other one, as screeches of merriment resounded round Howth Head. There were other, more intimate moments to be stored in the treasure-house of memory, as the day when both shared a bottle of Beaujolais and Vienna roll as the *Sea Scamp* bobbed on the quiet waters. The simplicity of the unexpected was now part of their lives.

If the fine summer weather retreated, still Howth held its fascination. Autumn walks were full of beauty. Sometimes they strolled along the sea-front watching the sulking sea hold an army of sailboats straining at the leash. Their sails were now furled, yet the clanking of loose-hanging cables made a music of their own. Larger fishing trawlers were ever-present, their tall masts lording it over the smaller craft.

On one misty evening they walked hand-in-hand up the hill, heading for Seagrave House. As Vicky looked at the figure striding towards them, she instantly recognised Gay Byrne, radio broadcaster and host of the well-known Late Late Show. Hugh was amused at her excitement, and after he bade "Good evening" to Mr Byrne, Vicky was walking on air. Puzzled, Hugh subsequently explained that Mr Byrne lived here, and often walked about in the evening. It was but one of a thousand occasions when he saw the little girl in Vicky, and wanted to protect her entirely.

Yet Vicky never once feared his attentions in those moments, for his fire was well in control. In fact, she sometimes wished that just a little more of the flame would fan forth, as she wouldn't have minded the scorch too much! However, what Vicky did not know was that Hugh, entirely attracted to her physical self, was at the same time acutely aware of their age difference, and so determined not to spoil their love affair by any precipitous move on his part.

ANOTHER autumn evening found Hugh in a painful quandary. The scene was a dinner party attended by himself, Vicky and another couple, both of whom were medical doctors. Proceedings began quite pleasantly, but the female doctor showed a growing curiosity concerning Vicky. She knew of Hugh's former wife Barbara, and at one point even remarked on Vicky being a "refreshing change of company". Nonetheless, she persisted in questioning Vicky at every lull in the conversation, and at one point even asked about Vicky's favourite authors. Though Vicky replied frankly that she had read little since leaving school, Hugh felt uncomfortable. With a discreet cough he pretended to have swallowed his wine too quickly, and rapidly re-directed the conversation. Indeed, several times throughout the meal he used similar tactics as he winced at Vicky's clear embarrassment.

Later that night when the guests had departed, Hugh drew Vicky to him and explained, "Don't worry darling. Kurt is a gentleman and a first-rate doctor, but he is kept under the thumb of that battle-axe. She rules the roost. I'm convinced that before they go anywhere, she plies him with drugs so that he loses his voice and she can thoroughly exercise that great throttle of hers. I love to meet Kurt on his own for a drink, but it's seldom he can do that." At that Hugh began mimicking the persistent chatterer and, true to form, Vicky rose above her deep hurt and laughed at length.

When Hugh returned after leaving Vicky home, his phone rang. Thinking it was Vicky, to his surprise he heard Kurt's voice saying, "Hugh, thanks for a lovely evening. Now listen, Hugh, I don't mean to interfere, but about that young lady, Vicky, she is rather young. I just hope you know what you're doing..."

Vicky wouldn't have believed Hugh capable of such an angry outburst, as he hollered into the mouth-piece. "Jesus Christ, Kurt, is it not quite enough to have to listen to that goddammed tongue-clacking woman of yours without having to listen to your worldly wisdom? Why can't you people mind your own goddammed business!" Slamming the phone down, he drew out a handkerchief and mopped his brow. Bewildered, he flopped onto the settee, where he was assailed by a plague of disquieting thoughts. No doubt that witch was rude and probing, and she clearly had no right to put Vicky through such agony. But, looking at things objectively, would it be fair to lead Vicky on if there was a real danger of their being incompatible? He reflected seriously on the age difference, the fact that he was twenty-six years on this earth before Vicky was born. Yes, he was utterly burning for her, but he must be sensible. He had met her friends from Brown Thomas. They were lively, intelligent, attractive, but there was an ocean of difference between the life of a beautician and that of a doctor of the mind. He couldn't think why but he was reminded of a delighted Vicky clicking her fingers to a tune as a dancer performed on television. Though she had a passing interest in more serious music, she wouldn't be the type to sit for hours listening to Chopin. And as that old dragon had so painfully shown, Vicky was not a very avid reader. Yet she had such an active mind and such a lively imagination. When she tried to describe something, she spoke more than eloquently with her hands and eyes. At that Hugh once more fell into a blessed daydream of the love of his life, determined to bid the world — including Kurt and his meddlesome goat of a wife — go hang.

Back home, a less confident Vicky lay awake for ages, her mind restless. She thought of the ordeal she had been through, yet actually felt more sorry for Hugh. How skilfully he protected her from the onslaughts of that wicked woman. Yet, a more threatening fear possessed her; namely, could she truly fit into the world of psychiatry, literature and classical music?

THAT Saturday Hugh pretended to be engrossed in writing, but only half of his attention was focussed on the matter in hand. The other half was captivated by a very curious, albeit grimacing Vicky, as she fingered the books stacked along several shelves in his study. The titles were off-putting, but from time to time she selected one for closer scrutiny. Hugh was quietly amused as she flipped through the pages, reading a passage or two and frowning. She was none too careful either in replacing the ones that she obviously disliked. Choosing one particularly heavy volume, she perched herself edgeways on Hugh's writing desk. At that, Hugh replaced the top of his fountain pen and gave her his undivided attention, just as he would a patient of his. As always her closeness stirred him, and swiftly drew him back into a more relaxed mode.

"Hugh, what the hell is a complex, in simple language?" Vicky finally spoke, gazing in disbelief at page upon page of utterly strange definitions.

"It's a hidden, unconscious force that compels people to think, feel or act in a certain way," Hugh replied without hesitation.

"Well, why in the name of God does this book take about a hundred pages to say just that?"

"Because in that way the writer can be very clever-sounding," Hugh chuckled, as an expression of annoyance appeared on Vicky's face, making him marvel that even being cross did not mar her exquisite features.

"Oh, I see! These psychiatrists like to make women appear silly and brainless!"

"Now come on, Vicky, there are nearly as many female psychiatrists as there are male."

Vicky released the volume into Hugh's open hand. He closed it and placed it on the far end of the desk, then reached around and with the his other hand drew Vicky over the desk and onto his knees. Again, her closeness was distracting, so Hugh pecked her cheek and grinned.

"Somehow, I think my Vicky is just a little itty bitty out o' sorts today. Maybe she should have a sign on her bed, telling her which side to get out of."

"It's just that I hate all this mystery about psychiatry. Just how exactly does it work?"

"O.K., in simple language you're my patient. Now you come to me in some distress. I listen to you in a most attentive manner as you pour out your heart to me. Then I say, 'Vicky, I'm afraid I've some bad news for you; you're acting like a long-tailed bob-cat at a rockin' chair convention, and you'll need to take a valium sandwich three times daily.'"

A laughing Hugh hugged Vicky. Pouting, she rose abruptly from his knees and faced the windows.

"Perhaps it's just that you psychiatrists don't know yourselves what you are talking about," she said coldly. Hugh walked over to her and placed his chin on her shoulder. "You know, you're dead right honey," he cooed. "I'll have to go to a shrink myself." He hunched his back in a grotesque fashion and with hands clasped on his head, craned his neck this way and that as he tottered around the study, calling out "Is there a psychiatrist in the house? Help — Hugh Osbourne Burke is in need of urgent assistance."

Once again Vicky managed to summon an air of mere tolerance. Conceding defeat, Hugh sat down and once more admired her trim figure outlined by the window. "She sure is a character," he thought, "quite ready to dislike what she perceives to be psychiatry." He wanted to laugh when he considered that in one fell swoop she had demolished his years of training and experience, but he decided that he would be wise to subdue himself. One thing for sure, she was showing herself to be a stubborn young lady. He longed to tell her how he really did love her when she was angry, but that might spoil the fun. Instead he walked over and turned her towards him, taking her two hands in his.

"Vicky, I'm giving a talk in the Shelbourne Hotel tomorrow evening, so I won't see you till later. I do hope my little spitfire can wait till then." Her eyes lighting up, Vicky looked like an excited little girl awaiting a big surprise. Placing her palms flatly on Hugh's chest, she asked, "Hugh, can I go?"

Hugh was taken aback.

"Now my little sweetie pie, what interest would you have in a talk on psychology? You'd be bored."

Vicky withdrew her hands and once more perched on the writing desk.

"What you really mean is that I wouldn't be able to understand a word. I'm only a cosmetics girl, so I'm supposed to be silly and feather-headed." Clearly shocked, Hugh spoke sharply to her, emphasising every syllable.

"Vicky, I never want to hear you say that again. That's utter nonsense." Vicky looked slightly alarmed at his outburst, as Hugh continued in a lower tone. "You are a very intelligent girl, Vicky, but I don't expect you to be an expert in psychiatry, and I sincerely hope you would not expect me to be knowledgeable of the world of cosmetics. We've been through this before. I love you, Vicky, for who you are. Do you understand that, Vicky? I love you."

As he stared imploringly into her eyes, she leaned her head towards him and said, "I'm sorry Hugh. I didn't mean to upset you. I do love you Hugh."

Hugh was smiling once more, shaking his head like an exasperated father. "Look, you can come," he drawled, "but don't blame me if a two-hour lecture on archetypes and the unconscious drives you clear out of your cotton-pickin' mind. You got my meanin'?"

Vicky clasped her hands round his neck and squealed in delight. When she settled down a little, Hugh flopped into his chair and said with a mock weariness, "Well, so much for psychiatry. You know Vicky, you could talk your way into selling the pyramids and promising to have them delivered by express mail. Poor, poor old Hugh," he moaned, only to be rewarded with a mischievous smile.

VICKY was amazed at the speed with which the conference room of the hotel filled. When Hugh had first mentioned the lecture, she imagined an audience of ten or fifteen. Now there were already about fifty present and people still filing in, so that the lecture started at ten minutes past eight to accommodate the latecomers. A hush descended on the audience as a smartly dressed lady appeared on stage to announce the speaker. Acknowledging the enthusiastic applause, Dr Hugh commenced with a confused expression. "Thank you, ladies and gentlemen. The title of this evening's lecture is...what is the title of this evening's lecture?" he stammered.

As a few unsuspecting souls near the podium helpfully murmured, "Archetypes and the Unconscious", Hugh smiled slightly. His opening jest set the tone for an exciting two hours, though not particularly for Vicky! At first she was conscious only of the fact that when he spoke, he scanned the entire audience, his eyes not especially dwelling on her. Try as she might to be sensible, she felt uneasy about this. If she really tried, she might have followed the main themes for the first hour, but her mind was not really so inclined. Instead she was taken up with the ages and variety of the people seated about her, most of whom occasionally laughed heartily at Hugh's quips.

At about nine o'clock Hugh announced a ten-minute break during which refreshments would be served. Hugh was handed a cup of tea. He beamed a smile at Vicky, who moved as if to join him at the foot of the stage. To her annoyance six or seven people had already encroached upon him. The most obvious was an elegantly dressed girl about Vicky's age. Vicky distinctly heard her excited voice, speaking French. Vicky had learned French at school but had forgotten it, having strongly disliked her French teacher! Still she was astounded at the fluency with which Hugh was responding, and a feeling of envy laced with jealousy possessed her. How dare this continental brim-hatted glamour puss be so obviously familiar! Someone spoke to Vicky, yet she barely heard the remark, "Isn't he a genius?" Turning, Vicky looked into the face of a young man in his early twenties.

"Yes," she replied absently, still eyeing the French girl who was now taking leave of Hugh.

"You know, we were lucky to get him for this lecture. Even the Freudians are screaming to get Dr Hugh to give a talk."

"Indeed," replied Vicky, cringing as Hugh kissed the girl goodbye.

The line of people wanting a word with Hugh was growing, so Vicky decided to wait till after the lecture to join him. The young man at her side meanwhile chatted on.

"You know, he has written extensively on the archetypes and general Jungian psychology. His books are best sellers in the States, and they'll be available here soon," he added excitedly. Then, noticing Vicky was in another world, he paused, slightly embarrassed. "Are you here on your own?" he asked awkwardly.

"No, I'm with Dr Hugh."

The young man changed course immediately. "Oh, are you an analyst?" With that, Vicky checked for the Exit sign, excused herself and headed for the door, leaving the young man mystified. Taking a seat in the hotel lounge, she ordered a pot of coffee, needing time to think.

An hour later she knew she had to share those thoughts with Hugh who, having had some difficulty finding her, was now upset to see her looking so worried.

"Hugh, we've got to talk."

"Okay, shoot," he sounded reassuring.

"Hugh, I never knew you were known to all those people, or that you were famous or anything like that. When you were speaking in there, I had no idea of what you were on about. I would have been humiliated if anyone in the hall wanted to discuss the lecture with me."

Hugh adopted a resigned attitude at first.

"Why in tarnation should it matter to anyone why you're not into psychology? How many of them would have an idea about cosmetics? Jesus, Vicky, don't put me through this again."

"Hugh, you can't get away from it. When we first met, none of that mattered. Everything was new. Now I'm beginning to realise that I don't belong to your world. I'm sorry Hugh. I'm so confused."

"We've been over this damn business time and time again, Vicky. For me to hear this is worse than having to drink sulphuric acid. Blasted psychology. Damn!"

Vicky sensed his anger rising, yet Hugh summoned all his will power to try and remain composed. It was cruelly difficult. Car keys in hand, he gestured to Vicky that he would drive her home.

No words were spoken. From time to time Vicky observed an agonised look on Hugh's tanned face. When they arrived at the bungalow, he turned off the engine. Staring through the windscreen, his hands tightened on the steering wheel.

"So this is it!" he finally said. "Jesus Christ, Vicky, if that's what you want, go ahead and have it your way. You're a strong girl, Vicky. You've come through some nasty storms in your life and you've survived them. I never dreamed that the opinions of other people would come between us."

" It's not about other people's opinions, Hugh," interrupted Vicky. "It's just that I couldn't fit into your world. We're so different. We're worlds apart."

Hugh was fit to explode, yet said nothing.

"I need some time to think, Hugh."

"You know Vicky, not for one second did I ever think such nonsense could drive us apart. I could have understood problems regarding the difference in our ages, but this is garbage."

Vicky felt an undeniable fear at Hugh's anger and at his seeming lack of understanding. Unable to think of what to say, she eventually blurted,

"Look, can I ring you when I've thought things through?"

"Sure, you just do that," Hugh said, sounding ice-cold. "It's something you'll have to sort out yourself."

That Friday night was a sleepless one for Vicky. She found it hard to believe she had spoken her mind and now regretted it. She spent the entire weekend in an exhausting soul-search, weighing her options of either staying with Hugh and braving it out, or simply acknowledging that their worlds were too far apart. If she dallied, Hugh might prove determined in his refusal to resume their relationship, for as she had sensed on Friday night, he was quite capable of digging in his heels. Yet if she rushed her decision, she might start a life with Hugh, only to suffer greatly for it. Her indecision was sheer torture, and by Sunday evening she was beginning to panic. She must, she thought, jump one way or the other. Breathing a prayer to her mother for guidance, she lifted the phone and nervously dialled Hugh's number.

"Hugh," she began when he answered, "I thought I'd ring you about what you said."

"All right, Vicky," Hugh responded, his voice well-modulated, for he did not want to pressure

Vicky at any cost, however great his pain might be.

"Hugh, I've spent all weekend trying to sort myself out. The truth is, Hugh, that I cannot live without you. I know I may find some things difficult, but I'd rather put up with that than lose you."

After a pause, Hugh finally spoke. "Vicky, you must be honest with me for both our sakes. Tell me on your word of honour if this is entirely, entirely your own decision?"

"It is, Hugh, I swear it."

"Very good! Then I can call over to you?"

"Of course, I'd love that."

Vicky felt an unbelievable weight lifted from her shoulders. If she were both comforted and unsettled by Hugh's steady tone, the fact that he was now on his way to her spoke volumes!

LOUISE looked at Vicky again, a furtively quizzical look. There was no doubt about it, something was amiss, apparent even in the way Vicky idly examined her manicure, so different from the vigorous flexing and light-hearted admiration of perfectly filed fingernails which characterized her better moments. What's more, all morning long her brightly alert welcome to customers had been replaced by a polite, minimal interaction. Clearly it was time to investigate this, and finally lunch-break came.

"No Louise — it's nothing really," Vicky answered her. "Things are really fabulous between Hugh and myself. He's just something else, everything I could ask for in a man. It's just..." suddenly her eyes filled up and Louise took her hand like a sister. Gradually it emerged that as she turned her calendar to October that morning, a certain date had darted from the columns and stuck in her heart. It was the twelfth of the month, her twenty-first birthday. She dreaded that day, her first birthday to celebrate without her mother. Louise understood and regretted having jested with Vicky earlier on.

Time kept up its daily pace, and the twelfth rolled on. When Vicky arrived that day at Brown

Thomas, it was clear some early morning tears had been shed. In the glove compartment of her car lay several birthday cards, not as many as usual because the old custom of not sending birthday cards for the first year of bereavement still prevailed. Those that she had opened were thoughtful, subdued gestures — mostly from her friends in Brown Thomas and in the squash club. The one from Brian in South Africa contained a long letter, which she would read later. However, as she had lifted the envelope bearing the Deutschland stamp, her heart had filled with an appalling dread. She had longed so much to open it, but feared the onslaught of a resentment, bordering on hatred, that no doubt would vie with long-ago love and cherished memories. Consequently her better judgement had advised her that if she opened it now, a torrent would be released that might prove uncontrollable. Better to wait, as a day's work lay ahead.

Once at Brown Thomas, however, Sophie and Louise as usual turned up trumps; always the right word, a gentle touch of humour, and when necessary a discreet silence.

An hour later found Vicky whispering to Sharon — Sharon who had accompanied her on her book-search, and Sharon who had designed a dress for Vicky that would have suited a goddess.

"I'm going out for a meal with him tonight, Sharon, up to Killakee House...no...nothing to do with my birthday, Sharon...but he did ask me to wear the blue dress. I couldn't let him know it was my birthday."

"Of course you couldn't!" said Sharon with a laugh.

"Who cares about birthdays anyhow!" mused Vicky that evening as she waited for Hugh to collect her, her spirits already lifting. Brian's letter had been fabulous, and the dreaded envelope with its German postmark could wait till she got home again. For now, Hugh was coming and the promise of a wonderful night lay ahead.

After starters, they regarded each other through the candle-light, and Vicky noted something of a roguish smile creeping across Hugh's face. Over his shoulder she saw what appeared to be a flower-arranging ceremony taking place, as an invisible waiter, hugging a large circular arrangement of red roses, was being guided by a younger chap. Suddenly the procession stopped at the table where Hugh and Vicky sat. A cascade of tears poured down Vicky's lovely face as Hugh said, with a trembling voice, "Happy Birthday darling!"

Vicky impulsively abandoned her seat to throw her arms around Hugh. The waiter and his assistant made brief adjustments to the huge bouquet, before deciding it was better to retreat. For several minutes silence reigned, broken only by muted, involuntary sobs where words would have intruded.

As the meal resumed, Vicky's curiosity only incited Hugh to further playful teasing, for she was positive she had not dropped the merest hint that it was her birthday. Eventually relenting, he told her he had asked Fiona. This was almost too much for Vicky — Fiona, the double agent who had furnished her with details about Hugh! When she told him of Fiona's dual role, he too was speechless, all of the happy intrigue only further flavouring their meal!

Back at Vicky's bungalow, Babycham played with Hugh's shoelaces, amusing them both. Still Vicky noticed that Hugh had gone silent, obviously preoccupied. With some hesitation he asked her to excuse him, while he went to the car. Once again so struck by his immaculate appearance, Vicky thought nothing of his request, admiring rather the smart grey suit that enhanced a body that was obviously fit and disciplined. Yet upon his return, Vicky grew curious, for he had gone past her into the kitchen, not quite concealing a white paper bag. Babycham, now tired out, suddenly jumped in shock as a sharp pop echoed throughout the quiet bungalow. Shortly after Hugh emerged with a radiant smile, holding two glasses and a bottle of champagne. After a suitable toast and clink of glasses, both sat on the settee. The clanking radiator beside them signalled comforting signs of heat, and Vicky unplugged the electric fire. Once more Hugh lapsed into a train of silent thought; then as if he had solved some problem, he put his hand into the pocket of his jacket and took out a red velvet-covered box. He opened it to reveal a pair of sapphire earrings on a shimmering satin cushion. Vicky was breathless. She wondered was the champagne playing tricks on her, for she literally could not speak. The right words were also eluding Hugh, who finally spoke.

"Vicky, I hope you like them. I could think of nothing that would go better with that blue dress, and those blue eyes. Vicky — I think you know how much I love you. I thought I knew what love was before, but you have invaded me, body and soul. Maybe I don't show it so much — for so long my very power to love has been on ice. Anyway..." he stumbled, "what am I trying to say?"

He took a deep breath as if to steady himself.

"I love you Vicky, more than I can tell. I have been praying night and day that our age difference will never force us to drift apart. That's all."

Vicky was ecstatic. Once more she threw her arms around him, the shoulder of his grey jacket growing damp with tears. She clung to him tightly, then releasing him, searched those deep brown eyes.

"Hugh, I love you, I love you, I love you. You will never, never grow old. My God, Hugh, if only you knew. My life is nothing without you."

Some hours later Hugh counted four milk-vans on his way back to Howth. Stepping out of his car at Seagrave House, he surveyed the dark expanse of sea, feeling the thin breeze of the approaching dawn. Then looking up to the heavens, he smiled, giving heartfelt thanks to the gods.

That next morning the letter opener shook repeatedly in Vicky's hand. She made an awkward incision, then placed the envelope back on the coffee-table, its contents untouched. When an hour later she rang Hugh, he was alarmed, for Vicky would not ring him at his consulting rooms in Fitzwilliam Square unless it was urgent. Relieved when she told him of her fear of reading her father's letter, he arranged to meet her in Davy Byrne's, a well established tavern in Duke Street.

Seated there, Hugh tried to show no emotion as he read the letter silently.

My Dearest Vicky,

My fondest love to you on your twenty-first birthday. I was saddened to learn of your mother's death, and I know it cannot be easy for you to celebrate your birthday on your own. And if I had my way that would not be the case... However, I assure you that my thoughts are with you.

I have two wishes Vicky, and you have the right to refuse them both, nor could I blame you. Firstly, I would give the world to come and see you, and I beg of you to allow me.

Secondly, and this may be harder for you Vicky — I want you to believe me that I never forgot you, and that not hearing from you has torn my very heart out. I had a dreadful decision to make, I know — one that crucified me. And not being able to see you only drove the nails further in and further tortured me.

I beg of you my dearest Vicky, please grant me these two wishes, which would give me paradise itself.

How I love you, my princess (I still think of that baby-name I gave you!) I look forward to your reply — please don't dash my heart on the stones.

Your ever-loving Dad

Hugh noted every word, his skill as a therapist coming into play. He contemplated Vicky, then spoke softly. "Vicky, your father very much wishes to see you. Yet the decision must be yours. Whatever course of action you take, I will support you one hundred percent."

He placed the letter in her hand, yet Vicky hardly saw the writing, as if too close a scrutiny would have revealed too much of the agony in the script.

For several days after Vicky was in turmoil, as her mind's eye focussed on the days of green parkland and ice-cream vans, compounded by the vision of her broken-hearted mother. There was also the discovery of the bundles of letters and birthday cards, and the more recent memory of Hugh playing *Für Elise*. Realising her dilemma, Hugh with infinite patience teased out various issues which might have remained hidden to her. And as he suspected, the forgiving side of Vicky's nature ultimately won out.

The hours preceding her father's arrival only eight days later proved painful indeed, as her memories absolutely took over. Was this the father who'd sat her on his knee and let her hold a lit match to his pipe? She pictured him cutting the plug tobacco in slices, then kneading it in his strong palms. She remembered how, with great skill, he filtered the finely ground flakes into the pipe until it was ready for lighting. And how the reddening tobacco would rise. When he gently tamped the burning material with his forefinger, she had always wondered how it did not hurt him. She remembered also how he showed her to make a penny "jump" from one hand into a paper bag, or how she had loved hiding somewhere when he came home in the evening. An immediate "search" would take place during which Linda would tell him Vicky must be lost. Then, having almost given up, he would pounce on the hiding child and throw his gaberdine over her so that he might never lose her again. She reflected sadly again on how, whenever possible, he had collected her from school, recognising the sound of his car pulling up outside, as not many children were driven home from school then. Even at the age of ten, she would go into ecstasy at the sound of that car, until sadly this great treat became a spasmodic affair, before ceasing altogether. This loss had hurt Vicky terribly, but not nearly as much as sitting at dinner and not having him there. Worst of all was going to sleep without his goodnight visit for a 'tuck-in' and a kiss. Even at such a tender age she had suspected somehow that he was also hurting her mother. And worst of all was that day in the park when he told her he must go away. That was the beginning of the end, followed by her Confirmation day, when she truly missed him once more. Bad as that was, however, it was nothing to her feeling of isolation and misery the night she was called to the hospital, only to find that Linda had passed away.

Seated awaiting him, Vicky found more immediate thoughts rushing through her mind. For example, what would he look like now? What will he think of her? What would Linda think of this meeting? And just what would they talk about, as certain topics would be unbearable.

When the doorbell finally rang, she rose, stricken, remembering those days when she had rejoiced on hearing her father turning his key in the lock. Managing to compose herself, she opened the door. Contrary to what she had imagined, she recognised Walter immediately, though how he had aged! In a split second Vicky's arms drew him towards her, and no words were said for several minutes as Vicky and her father shook in tearful embrace.

What conversation ensued was laboured but deeply moving. Yet Vicky could do little to ease her father's burden as he explained why he had not come for Linda's funeral.

"Vicky, deep down I was terrified that in your grief you would reject me, nor could I have blamed you. I was a fool Vicky. I had everything a man could wish for, and threw it away. Things never worked out with the other woman, and how often I resolved to ask your mother's forgiveness face to face, yet when the time came I weakened."

As he reflected bitterly on his departure from the home in which he now sat, Vicky felt great pity for him. In some confusion she realised that as a child she took it for granted that her father knew everything, that he was the one person above all who could bring order and meaning into chaos. Yet by not returning to beg forgiveness of her mother, he had blighted his own life, as well as Linda's and Vicky's.

Vicky tried to fill him in on the years following his departure, a difficult if not impossible task. It would have been easier to dwell on her younger years, but that would have proved excruciating for them both. When she told him about Hugh, however, he was greatly consoled by her account of him. Placing an arm around her, he whispered with powerful emotion, "Vicky darling, I never forgot you — not for a single day." With that, Vicky broke down once more, before going to her bedroom to return clutching a bundle of cards tied with red satin ribbon.

Hugh timed his arrival perfectly, father and daughter having been re-united for two hours. One look at Vicky told of a river of tears, and Hugh also noted how watery ink had seeped across her father's white knuckles, as Walter sat clutching the ten birthday cards. It was a heart-wrenching scene that culminated when Walter spied his own photo, still taking pride of place in the home he had abandoned.

Before departing, father and daughter embraced for a long tearful moment. Hugh was then clasped in a manful embrace, only to hear a heartfelt whisper, "Take care of her, Hugh, take care of her." Promising himself that he would do just that, Hugh walked Vicky slowly back to her bungalow door.

As the emotional turmoil of her father's visit gradually subsided over the next week, one fact emerged quite clearly for Vicky. Namely, if she had forgiven Walter, she had also quite clearly lost him. Yet if nothing could make good his absence during those tumultuous years, Vicky sensed that she might now be able to set aside some of that overwhelming emptiness within that had so often beset her since he had deserted her.

HOWTH in autumn would challenge the greatest artists, as here and there strong winds gathered clusters of fallen leaves. Intrigued by Vicky's bright imagination, Hugh listened as she explained that this frenzied activity was once believed to be the work of meddlesome fairies, her description so vivid that he could almost see them in their thousands swirling their brooms. Likewise gazing at the broad expanse of surging waves, he recalled Vicky describing the thousands of white horses who pounded the ocean deep, tossing their white manes. Clearly she had thrown a new identity on this old Viking haunt for Hugh.

Weekends they trudged the crispy foliage of October and later the cold, mucky underfoot puddles of November. Their pace increased with the onset of the colder, wetter weather, yet the camouflage of white rain-gear and smart black riding boots could not disguise Vicky's smile and bubbling spirits. Like Hugh, she too found a sense of adventure in the moodiness of Irish winter weather.

Even without the very efficient heating system, Seagrave House might have proved a fortress against the fiercest of winter's chilling draughts. Moreover, Hugh had added a homely, simple touch, spending hours driving an axe through the trunk of a fallen tree, and soon building up a stock-pile of neatly split logs for the woodshed. Perhaps a streak of frontier spirit still lurked in his Yankee blood? In any case Vicky would never forget the long hours curled up on the settee with him, the crackling of the fire their only companion. She always hated when it was time for leaving, and Hugh sensed something of this. The deteriorating December weather did not help matters, nor did the resumption of their working week. Yet if Hugh detested returning home to Seagrave House without her, he did not wish to force her in any way, nor force the pace of their as yet unconsummated love affair.

Meantime the Christmas spirit had overtaken Brown Thomas by storm. Back at work, Vicky looked around in wonder as she prepared her counter for busy days ahead. As was her way, she easily imagined how busy sprites had overnight swung out of the chandeliers to weave glistening strings of tinsel into corners that looked utterly inaccessible. The Brown Thomas Christmas tree itself stood tall, bearing a display of flickering lights, while bunches of golden-sprayed fir cones peeped out at the early shoppers, midst sprigs of holly and berries shimmering at every angle.

The days leading up to Christmas were hectic, and extra staff were employed to cope with larger crowds of customers. Male shoppers were in particular a source of steady amusement to the cosmetic girls. So reticent, they often hovered around the counters for ages before presenting themselves for service. Vicky cried with laughter when Louise whispered that some of them would no doubt die of fright, had they to purchase certain items from the lingerie department! Still, even her lovely Hugh could not manage that.

Zoë herself had come in to help for the Christmas period. If no ambulance-taxis arrived for her this time, something else alarming was bound to happen with Zoë around. Indeed one day a very distressed messenger informed the cosmetic section that a lady had fallen on the stairs and broken her leg. Zoë gathered from him that the unfortunate soul was the very woman she could see across the way, sitting on a chair, and quite clearly unable to move. Immediately Zoë shouted to Louise to ring for an ambulance, while she signalled a security guard, knowledgeable in first aid, who dashed to the rescue. Reassuring the lady seated on the chair, he insisted she should not attempt to move her leg, whose leather boot lay on the floor beside her. The security guard deftly probed the leg with skilled fingers, only to be

literally knocked speechless as the offended lady
pushed him violently aside, inquiring in an
outraged voice had he gone entirely mad? It
seemed Zoë's hysterical instructions had led the
poor guard to a customer who had merely asked
for a chair to remove her new boots which were
pinching her. Meanwhile the real victim of the fall
was already being stretchered out to the
ambulance.

Christmas Eve when it arrived had all the signs
of ushering in a white Christmas, as the sky
increasingly filled up with slate gray leaden
clouds. Lunch-time in Davy Byrne's was cosy, as
the cosmetic girls sat in a circle. Gentle strains of
Christmas carols fused with the babbling of the
clientele, and if the girls were aware of Vicky's
frequent silences, they were by now also well
aware that the object of her deep thoughts was a
gloriously happy one.

During the late afternoon Vicky's total attention
seemed to swing between two distinct points, her
watch, and the main entrance of the store. Then,
five minutes before closing time, Brown Thomas
staff and passers-by were stopped in their tracks
at the sight of her being swung around by a six-foot
plus American, as her coat and suitcase sat nearby.

In her confusion, Vicky stammered to Hugh that she must wish the girls a happy Christmas. Amused, Hugh smiled as she dashed from counter to counter. Preparing to leave, Hugh drew her to him as if to protect her against the cold outside, while Louise and Sophie looked on in wonderment. Understanding at once that age was truly irrelevant, they were also highly amused at the fact that Vicky was leaving five minutes before her time! Yet there was no point in telling her, as clearly she was now well and truly beyond the constraints of space and time!

IT was a great relief to take shelter in the Mercedes, where Vicky could savour an inner glow. Hugh had asked her to spend Christmas in Seagrave House, the invitation given several days previously. Vicky giggled quietly to herself when she recalled the occasion; Hugh had grown tongue-tied half way through, and Vicky nearly had to come to his assistance. Ultimately both of them burst into a laughter of relief, capping an exquisite moment. Now, this evening, she did not even mind leaving Grafton Street with its throngs of busy shoppers and its throbbing Christmas heart.

Hugh negotiated the Howth road which skirted a dark and unfriendly sea, while what at first seemed to be a light snow shower rapidly closed in. Soon the snowflakes increased in size and number, until eventually Hugh had to reduce speed as a full-blown blizzard rapidly thickened the white blanket that formed round about. It was comforting to swing into the driveway of Seagrave House, though Hugh pretended not to notice Vicky's excitement on seeing a magnificent Christmas tree in the garden. Its multi-coloured, flickering lights made a striking contrast to the darkening sky and the fresh snow. Through the car's windscreen the coloured fairy-lights developed long, needle-like silvery tails. An older woman wearing a white apron opened the door. She barely greeted Dr Hugh, but gave Vicky a thorough "once-over" before inviting her to take off her coat. Hugh briefly introduced Vicky to Nora, then excused himself as he left to prepare drinks. "Gonna be a lotta shakin' an' mixin' in here for a while," he joked before going out. In fact he had an extraordinary repertoire of cocktails from which he loved to surprise Vicky. As he retired to the next room a wave of superb cooking aromas pervaded the atmosphere, before Nora closed the door at Hugh's request.

Nora sat down near Vicky, and pulled her by the sleeve so she would not have to raise her voice.

"He's such a beautiful gentleman — real quality ma'am. I do the odd day for him — like — I often do the bit of cooking or cleaning."

She leaned even closer to Vicky. "When the little boy was killed, his heart split in two. After Barbara, the wife, went off, I used to worry myself sick about him. She must have been a hard woman, ma'am. He'd stand there for hours just gazing out at the sea. Never once did he open the piano or play a record. Then about five months ago he started to pick up. When I heard him singing to himself one morning, I said to meself — the doctor is coming back to himself — nothing surer. He was singing that thing *Carrickfergus* — it sounded so funny in that American accent of his."

She clutched Vicky's sleeve even tighter, and went on. "It was prayers, ma'am. I prayed that he'd come back to himself or that God would take him out of his misery. He doesn't go to Mass — you know, ma'am — but don't get me wrong — he's a good man, and he's supposed to be a brilliant man for them sufferin' from the nerves. The nerves is an awful curse ma'am."

The one-sided chatter went on in low tones, Vicky spell-bound as Nora told how she had prayed that God would send Hugh a nice, quiet woman to comfort him, how he'd be a very kind husband, repeating that he'd only started to smile again in the past five months. Vicky did not know what to say in reply, and was greatly relieved when Hugh re-appeared, carrying two tall cocktail glasses with cherries, cream and umbrellas crowning them. Declining a brandy, Nora explained to Dr Hugh that she had an ocean of work to do, before rushing back to the kitchen.

"Nora is a real topper," laughed Hugh. "I bet by now she knows your seed, breed and pedigree, Vicky, but she means well. Trouble is, there are times she thinks she's my mother. She'd have been flipping mad if I hadn't introduced you!"

Vicky was highly amused, and all the more idolised this unassuming giant. If this Christmas Eve was largely sheer ecstasy, one black cloud briefly loomed on the horizon. As Vicky was admiring the large satin-covered Christmas card she had sent to Hugh, propped now at the base of a beautifully trimmed tub that held the tree, her gaze fell on another card, not quite as large as hers. Straining, she could just could make out the word *Barbara* and several *xxxx*. Though the initial shock was great, Vicky was determined not to let imagination spoil this lovely night. Anyway, it was not Hugh's fault if Barbara had sent a card like this, and Hugh had too lofty a mind to leave it undisplayed. Thus, any fleeting hurt she may have felt had dissipated before it came time to retire. Hugh held her tightly to him as they stood outside her room. Never before had she felt so close to him, never before had he wanted her so much. Clearly both of them suffered great pangs of longing, and it was equally clear that neither of them could hold back much longer.

A knock on the bedroom door the next morning awakened Vicky. Hugh laid the breakfast tray on the press near her bedside. "Happy Christmas, darling," he bent and kissed her.

Howth was never a noisy place, but this Christmas morning, an utter stillness had descended. Both Hugh and Vicky feasted their eyes on the whiteness all around. The Christmas tree in the garden bowed its outstretched arms with the weight of the clinging snow. The milkman had been late, his tell-tale double-trail of footprints still clear. Hugh waited till Vicky had finished breakfast and removed the tray.

Vicky's heartbeat stopped for a giddy second as she unwrapped the present Hugh handed her. It was a gold bracelet studded with a sapphire stone, and he mentioned modestly that it would match her earrings. With equal anticipation he unwrapped her present for him, and the leather-bound volume of Irish antiquities absolutely gladdened his heart. It was perfectly obvious that it was an expensive gift, but it was rather the thought that she had gone to the trouble of choosing it for him that launched his soul on a sea of gladness.

A ring on the doorbell at mid-morning heralded the arrival of an old friend of Hugh's. Father James had studied psychology with Hugh in Harvard, before deciding to become a priest. Studying his pale, ascetic form as Hugh introduced him, Vicky almost burst out laughing, as suddenly she remembered the first male teacher in her convent school. The girls had christened him "Bones" because of his lack of human flesh, and Father James could well share his nickname. Composing herself, Vicky tried to join the conversation, but she chilled inside at the thought of his cold handshake. She was also painfully conscious of the fact that he had betrayed signs of shock at first seeing her, and that he did not really include her in the conversation despite Hugh's tactful efforts to involve her. Even a hot whiskey by the blazing log-fire did little to thaw him out. When he departed, Vicky knew deep down that Hugh was hurt, but she was determined that goodwill should reign supreme. Still, she shared her memories with Hugh, and Hugh himself doubled up at the thought of an abnormally tall, gaunt teacher trying to impress fourteen-year-old schoolgirls with the intricacies of French grammar. He could well imagine Vicky then, all sweet and nice to the poor man's face, while all the time inventing such a dreadful name for him.

"Perhaps he had no hot water bottle last night, honey," drawled Hugh, as it was Vicky's turn to collapse into helpless laughter. Both of them sat on the rug opposite the cherry log fire. When Hugh passed dry remarks like these, Vicky's sense of humour responded immediately, and this one-liner had her in mortal danger of suffocating. Still Hugh decided it was not the appropriate time to explain to Vicky that Father James had undergone an experience some years back which had thrown his life as a priest into disarray. It concerned a young lady Father James had befriended, only to become more involved than he had bargained for. In fact he was on the point of leaving the priesthood when the young lady lost her nerve. The whole affair had traumatised him, and his subsequent recovery bore the hallmarks of a new fanaticism. A crusader now for every cause that came to his notice, he was noted for his black and white views on contraception and abortion, not to mention marital relationships!

That afternoon the extent of Nora's culinary skills was amply evident on the Christmas spread. Several glasses of wine enhanced the festive treat, and Christmas evening passed very quickly. More than once, Hugh replenished the glowing open fire. As night fell, Hugh and Vicky lapsed into a state of pleasant intoxication.

Later, in the small hours of morning, they stood on the landing once again, locked in an empassioned embrace. Vicky leaned back slightly, and with her arms still twined around Hugh's neck, looked into his eyes. "Hugh, I love you, I love you." A passionate kiss ensued, her tongue darting in an avid frenzy. Pausing, she whispered mockingly into his ear. " Do you want a hot water bottle tonight, Hugh?" Pausing only to nibble his ear lobe in a most sensuous manner, once more the tip of her tongue explored the deepest alcove of Hugh's ear.

Together they walked to Hugh's bedroom, arms about each other's waist. Conscious of the sinewy movement of his lean stomach, Vicky found it heavenly to be so close to him. Hugh was aware only of her trim, youthful hips causing his arm to move in unison with her firm footsteps. Overall it was almost too much to bear, for he was nearly delirious with desire. Upon entering Hugh's room, Vicky sensed a certain happy mystique. Although the main item here was an elegant double bed, the room had a distinctly masculine touch. Cleanliness reigned, but orderliness took second place. Two pillows lay on top of each other; two drawers lay open as if awaiting inspection. A cluster of books stood on the floor at the foot of the bed; one of his pipes leaned against the bedside lamp stand. It was as if she saw in these few seconds, Hugh, the impulsive teenager, for whom keeping a room tidy was tedious and boring. Yet she loved him for it all the more. For a split second she considered the former co-occupant of that double bed, but then firmly set that thought aside.

Standing by the bed, Hugh found his fingers trembling as he undid the buttons of Vicky's white silk blouse. Her firm breasts stirred visibly through the floral-patterned white bra, as if they craved his touch. In fact every nerve ending of her young body ached for him. It was then Hugh's turn to hold his breath as Vicky undressed before him. Truly she had not intended it to resemble a strip-tease, but every movement seemed one of sheer exultation. Hugh had to control his longing as she laid each garment carefully on a nearby chair, until she stood completely naked, then slipped between the sheets, watching avidly as Hugh's muscular body was revealed. As she ardently pulled him towards her, Vicky suddenly felt a resistance, and Hugh turned onto his back. Both hurt and puzzled, she heard him speak.

"Vicky, are you sure you won't regret this? You know I love you more than anything in this world — you know you're the only one I love — I just want to be sure that this is what you really want."

"My God, Hugh, of course I'll never regret it. If only you knew how much I need you Hugh — not just that great mind. I want you Hugh. I hunger for you. I hunger for your body and soul. Christ, Hugh, I am a woman!"

To Hugh's ecstatic delight, she reached across him to turn off the bedside lamp. Her sweet-scented hair fell away over his forehead, as her stiffening nipples brushed his face. His restraint heretofore had been phenomenal, but now his loins were tortured with a throbbing that screamed for release, as he realised he was nearly beyond the threshold of control. Vicky cried out with abandonment as he entered her, making Hugh understand only then that the intensity of her desire was as powerful as his.

As their lovemaking reached its passionate consummation, Hugh realised Vicky was indeed all woman, and consequently her need of him was all the more urgent. Still, for him the "little girl" quality in Vicky, combined with this newly realised sensuousness, only made her all the more utterly desirable.

When dawn broke on Howth Head, Vicky awoke, aware of Hugh's strong arm still embracing her. If only every night of her life could be like that Christmas night! It had been a night of intense abandoned passion, and this morning she could have shouted with uncontrollable joy that she had given herself to Hugh. She felt him move, reaching over to gently brush her unkempt hair back over her forehead. "Hugh — Hugh — please never leave me!" she murmured in response.

"My precious," replied Hugh, "I could not bear the very thought. Of course I will never leave you. It will never be that way."

FOR almost two hours they lay in a blissful dreamy state of togetherness. Gradually voices in the distance drew nearer and louder. There were sounds of excitement, cries of delight, a happy medley of noise. Vicky put on a pink, silk negligee and stood at the window. The scene beyond could have been cut from a Christmas card. Further falls of snow had merged road with footpath, along which a man was warding off snowballs thrown by his two young sons, their excited laughter bringing bittersweet thoughts to Vicky's mind. In fact, she felt pangs of sorrow whenever she thought of young Karl, and how Hugh must miss him at this season. Hugh was already standing behind her, his arms encircling her, his hands resting on either side of the window frame. His hand touched Vicky's, and a quick glance confirmed her fear. In that brief moment she saw in Hugh's face a terrible sadness, and as he swallowed hard, Vicky wished that she herself could bear his pain for him.

"I am a wounded healer," he finally spoke. "A wounded healer, Vicky. Please forgive me." As Vicky drew him to her, Hugh wept. After a minute or so he rubbed his eyes and forced a smile. "This is unnecessary; I must learn to live with my memories, the bad as well as the good."

"Look, let me get you some coffee," he added. "You're getting cold in that flimsy garment."

Immediately Vicky protested, insisting that she would serve him. But Hugh had won the battle against sad memories, and as if to confirm that, he solemnly pointed to the bed. "In you get, young lady, and be quick about it, doctor's orders!" Laughing, he pulled the duvet up about her chin, tucked her in, kissed her forehead and departed. A happy Vicky heard him humming as he headed for the kitchen, rekindling the mood of mutual joy in each other's company.

When they had finished their coffee, Hugh placed the empty cups and side plates on a nearby dressing table. As he returned to the bed, Vicky was chuckling, for a crust of toast had fallen into the sheets. She pursued it with her fingertips, but this action only drove it further down. Hugh's face lit up with his rogueish smile, as he slid in beside her, making her scream with laughter as he made frantic efforts to retrieve the crust, as if trying to catch a scurrying mouse. Vicky gave a sudden squeal as the sharp particle stuck into the soft flesh of her bottom. Finally catching hold of the offending item, she showed it to Hugh, who placed it near the bedside lamp and whispered into Vicky's ear, "My poor little baby, shall I make it better for you?"

"Ah, but then I'd have to show you where your little baby hurts," Vicky giggled. She nestled her head closer to Hugh, and with feather-like movements her fingers wandered over his chest, barely touching the very tips of his hair. As her breasts began to tingle, she turned more fully towards him and he towards her. His own arousal was as immediate and overwhelming, as the tips of her fingers continuously rippled over his body with tortuous lightness, and Vicky gasped in pleasure as he sought the furnace that pulsed waves of heat along her sensitive inner thighs.

Later, as they lay in each other's arms, passion spent but still smouldering, Vicky suddenly clutched his shoulders in what he realised was the gesture of a frightened child.

"Hugh, this is just like a magic dream — a dream I never want to waken from. But I sometimes imagine you meeting someone else or getting tired of me. That is the worst thing that could ever happen to me, I could cope with anything else, but that would be like a death to me, Hugh." The slow tone of his reply when it came almost burst her heart with joy. "You know, Vicky, maybe I should just examine that spot where the crust did its injury, if only to give you a good spanking for even thinking such a thing."

Vicky lay in a glorious trance, hardly aware that Hugh had been absent for almost twenty minutes, having arranged the cups and plates on the tray and carried them down to the kitchen. She was awakened from her reverie, however, by his reappearance in a bathrobe and sandals.

Smiling so innocently, without warning he reached down and lifted the unsuspecting Vicky first into his arms, then over his shoulder. She kicked and screamed but even in her nakedness her protests were of far more of joy than any complaint! Laughing, Hugh marched towards the bathroom carrying the helpless Vicky, who did not resist as he laid her in the bath.

There, a lather of scented suds caressed her as he gently sponged her. Glorying in his total possession of her, she occasionally flung a handful of suds at Hugh. Finally she stood unashamedly before him, glistening droplets still adorning her firm young breasts. With the most tender of touches, he slowly draped a large soft white bath towel around her and lifted her out. It seemed fitting that the bathroom windows were densely steamed.

RESUMING work after the Christmas holiday is never particularly easy for the majority of workers, but this season Vicky was a notable exception. Her steps along Grafton Street were light and surprisingly swift, and now and then she was tempted to pinch herself to test if her memories of Christmas were indeed real. Indeed she even failed to answer a few morning greetings from fellow walkers, as her mind still lingered on a superb Christmas day, followed by a night of passion. She pictured Hugh's constant trips to the woodpile and his subsequent strategic placing of the hissing logs on the blazing fire. A passer-by would have understood the reason for her lingering smile if he could have seen Vicky and Hugh tobogganing down a snowy slope, Hugh shouting instructions and Vicky screaming louder than the children about them, whenever her sled took up too much momentum.

Children — that reminded her of something! Following an afternoon of such winter sport, Vicky had chatted to Nora who was preparing the evening meal in the kitchen, while Hugh chopped logs into firewood. Vicky, now accustomed to Nora pulling her by the sleeve to whisper, was commenting on the children who had gathered in

Seagrave's garden that afternoon for the building of a huge snowman. Occasionally Vicky had urged one of the children to take a pot shot at the snowman, or at Hugh, the master of ceremonies, who would feign a mad dash after the offender. She was amused by the fact that these children addressed him simply as Hugh.

"You know, ma'am, it did me heart good to see the children there today," Nora looked round for unseen listeners. "Ever since little Karl's death, neither chick nor child has entered them gates. Mind you, I don't mean to talk out of place ma'am, but that Barbara one didn't like poor Karl's friends comin' here. You see, the doctor would be trick-actin' with them, an' that Barbara one was a bit too uppity for that. I never saw that one smilin' even once. God, Ma'am, it was smashin' to see the kids today — an' yourself ma'am, if you don't mind me mentionin' it. There's nothin' surer, the Doctor is comin' back to 'imself."

Vicky was about to thank Nora for the roundabout compliment when she felt an urgent tug at her sleeve.

"You know, ma'am, when you're in the vicinity at all — not meanin' to speak out o' place ma'am — it's like he gets a new meanin' to life. He's the real Doctor Hugh — laughin' singin' an' foolin' around. You've no idea, ma'am!!"

Nora's knowing smile was by now so familiar to Vicky, who smiled herself in delighted blushing confusion. As Hugh returned with more logs, Nora shouted like a practiced actress after Vicky who was now leaving the kitchen, "And a touch of garlic, ma'am, though too much will spoil it."

THAT morning the staff at Brown Thomas felt besieged. Any moment now, the doors would open, and a host of bargain-hunters would catapult into the various departments for the after-Christmas sales. Yet that was the least of Vicky's thoughts as Louise and Sophie made sly innuendos about her Yuletide visit to Howth. Vicky took it well; in fact she enjoyed the slagging. Later, when the rush of shoppers had eased somewhat, she confided in them that for the first time in her life she really knew love. Her two friends sat in a dream-like trance over coffee as she told them about Seagrave, her first white Christmas, and her wonderful Christmas present. As she spoke, her words of praise for "her Hugh" revealed the deepest conviction.

The new year unfolded, and early February found Vicky visiting Dr Henderson, whose voice seemed to be miles away, though he sat right across from Vicky. Only a mahogany desk bearing a blood pressure cuff separated them, but Vicky hardly heard his words of caution and common sense, conscious only of the fact that she was pregnant. Heaven had poured out the ultimate drops of its rapture, and her heart overflowed with happiness. Even if it killed her, she would not tell

Hugh until evening, though he would be somewhat later in collecting her, since he was preparing for an important conference. What he had not told Vicky was that he himself was the principal speaker, and that many of those attending were coming especially to hear him.

Walking on air, Vicky prepared her counter for the afternoon. While she simply burst to break the good news to Sophie and Louise, she must not do so, since Hugh should know first. Just imagine — Hugh Junior. While Hugh had insisted they not make love again until they married, Vicky was certain that he too would be delighted by her news. Her flying thoughts were suddenly anchored, though, by a distinctly American accent which inquired, "Are you Victoria Vaughan?"

A puzzled Vicky answered "Yes?" If she had never seen this lady before, her appearance was one not easily forgot: somewhat taller than Vicky, sallow skin, almond-shaped brown eyes, and auburn hair.

"I'm Barbara Whittaker," the woman spoke again. "I'm Hugh's wife."

Vicky felt as if a sledgehammer had hit her, only then remembering the photo in Seagrave House.

"I would be ever so thankful if I could meet you for a short time this evening — it's just something private I'd like to discuss — it's really important."

Envisioning the Christmas card emblazoned with "kisses", Vicky heard herself agree to meet Barbara in the Shelbourne Hotel at 6.30 p.m.

The Shelbourne Hotel had much in common with Brown Thomas. Both boasted a sense of timelessness, together with a conservative decor bearing the imprint of skilled craftsmanship, which issued a subtle invitation just to dally there. Yet all of this was utterly lost on Vicky. Even the superb coffee did nothing to revive her as she listened to Barbara Whittaker, who explained how she had decided to attend the forthcoming psychiatric conference.

"I've been in touch with Father James, Hugh's friend from Harvard days," Barbara added, "and thus was able to contact you." Vicky felt a strange and unpleasant sensation ripple down her spine at the mention of that Christmas morning visitor, which certainly didn't help her concentrate on Barbara Whittaker's words.

"I deeply appreciate your meeting me, Victoria. I realise that you think you are in love with Hugh," she said to Vicky, who was too numbed even to put that right! "I cannot blame you," Barbara continued. "Hugh is a wonderful, wonderful man. We were happy, Victoria, until tragedy struck. We lost our eight-year-old son, Karl. He was killed — because of a bicycle."

She waited till she could control her breathing, then continued. "The truth is that I blamed Hugh. I had never wanted him to get that bicycle, and we'd argued over it. From the moment we received the dreadful news of Karl's death until the day I left, I blamed him to a point where it poisoned my mind. After I settled back in America, however, I gradually saw that Hugh did not deserve my hatred. I could not sleep, Victoria, thinking of the torment he had suffered — weeks without eating, nights without rest, uninterrupted hours of standing at the window looking at the sea — as if he might see Karl on the horizon. In fact he wore a path to the cemetery where he cried alone. Even then, Hugh would not risk upsetting me by showing me his bleeding heart. I should never have left him, Victoria. It was the greatest mistake of my life. I fully understand your being involved with Hugh, as any woman would fall for him. I'm a psychologist myself, yet I even disliked his having female patients. I never trusted his secretaries nor his students. I tried to steer Hugh clear of women, but I see now that was an insult to his integrity. Victoria — I'm telling you, you are looking at a broken woman."

In fact Vicky was not looking at Barbara at all. Rather she was locked in a state of peripheral vision, aware only of her utter shock.

"I will not try to take him from you," Barbara resumed. "Indeed I'm begging you, Victoria, not even to let him know that I've spoken to you. However, I'm pleading, pleading that if he shows any sign in the next few days at the conference that he would be willing to forgive my rejection, please don't stand in the way of our re-uniting."

Had Vicky been her usual sprightly self, she would have seen before her the face of a woman haunted by guilt and grief. Instead she felt as if she had been thrown into an angry black torrent, its spewing foam dancing in mockery at her short-lived happiness. Still it was unthinkable that she should part from Hugh — death itself would be a better option! She pictured the harrowing scene of leaving forever from his comforting arms, picturing Hugh's own tortured face. Suddenly that image was replaced by a scene from her childhood days: she was coming home from school, her dad having collected her that particular day. A screech of brakes rang out, followed by the sound of metal being scraped along the concrete, as her father released her hand and dashed across the road. In a second he was huddling over what appeared to be a ragged doll drenched in blood. She remembered Gardai pushing onlookers away and ambulance doors being slammed. Her father tried unsuccessfully to comfort her, but she wondered why he would not let her go to see what could be done with the tangled bicycle. Later, she ate her dinner, not quite understanding why he had only a cup of tea. Then, with a terrifying jolt, she realised that this memory had uncannily depicted exactly what Hugh and Barbara had experienced, almost exactly how they had lost Karl! Once again she pictured Hugh's agony as he stood motionless for hours on end staring out to the sea in vain, as if hoping for a miracle, his lonely treks to the cemetery, even Nora's fears for his very sanity. Barbara, too, had obviously suffered a similar acute anguish, though she showed it in an entirely different way.

"O God," Vicky breathed. It was a passionate prayer that all this might prove a foul trick of imagination, but reality beat on without mercy. Gradually she steeled herself to entertain thoughts of the very worst that could happen; yet knowing full well that losing Hugh would leave her desolate, the mere thought of it terrified her. And yet, through this darkest of nightmares, one tiny bright flame shone through; no matter what destruction fate might dispense, nobody — nobody — nobody could take from her this precious part of Hugh's very essence that she now carried within.

Later that evening, Vicky replaced the telephone with a trembling hand, having rung Hugh to tell him she was feeling unwell, and that she would see him the following night.

HUGH presumed that Vicky's reason for not meeting him that night was genuine, as apart from her odd practical jokes, she had never lied to him. Still there had been just the tiniest hint of hesitancy in her voice. Dismissing it, he decided to devote some time to reading. Just as he settled into his favourite chair at the bay-window, the phone rang. If he seldom received calls at Seagrave, he certainly didn't expect to hear Barbara's voice. Come to think of it, she hadn't been at the last few lectures of the conference, though when they had met, their relationship had seemed comfortable enough. Accordingly Hugh saw no reason for refusing her request to see him, thinking Vicky would understand. Yet he was a little taken aback, when Barbara suggested that instead of meeting somewhere in the city, she would make her way to Seagrave.

Clearly so much had changed. There had been a time when Hugh would have been waiting at the door long before she arrived, but now, staring at the closed door, Barbara felt somewhat like an intruder. Everything lovely about Howth now seemed like an instrument of torture, and even the magnificent expanse of evening sea leered at her. The very name Seagrave taunted her, while the crystal water fountain in the garden seemed to trickle in a human whisper, "Too late — too late!" Noticing three circles of bright border flowers surrounding its base, she realised with suppressed outrage that these were a new addition.

While Hugh greeted her with a quiet, courteous welcome, she could not deny a secret sense of satisfaction when he told her that Vicky wouldn't be around that evening. Yet her first step into the hallway once again brought home the stunning stark reality of Karl's absence, which once again wrenched her heart, and rendered her speechless. It seemed Hugh understood, and gently seating her, he prepared a cool drink. His kindness however did nothing to ward off emotions that terrified her, such as her wish to lash out at the hand that had rearranged Karl's photo, placing it between two silver vases with fresh flowers. If that was most certainly a woman's touch, there were other distinctly feminine imprints on this room; what about the finely cut white lace cloth that lay on the piano-top, the matching covers on the armchairs? And Hugh certainly did not buy that pipe-rack on the coffee table. Still, she had better stifle these feelings for the moment, or her venture would be doomed to failure. As it was, she barely heard Hugh suggest that it might be helpful, if she felt up to it, to visit Karl's grave.

The cemetery was peaceful as two silhouetted figures appeared against the clear evening sky. The loving care which had been lavished on Karl's grave was evident, and while Hugh supported Barbara, once again the silent tears of those two who had adored their only child poured onto the lonely plot. Their eyes lingering on the tombstone, Hugh squeezed Barbara's arm, as one last time she ran her palm slowly over the top of the marble stone before kissing it. Hugh tried to prevent her from looking back, but when she did, she saw the tombstone standing in unrepentant defiance.

Barbara tried her utmost to be cheerful for the remainder of the evening, but Seagrave was as quiet as the cemetery. Over the meal, it had been quite impossible for her to spell out the true reason for her visit, and she now sat with Hugh on the settee they had so often occupied in happier times, though Barbara was painfully aware of the fact that he did not reach for her hand and pull her onto his lap. Oh, for times past! she thought as several times she stole glances at the man she loved, more so now than ever. He had not changed, still that strong, calm, young man she had met at Harvard. If he had never been at ease speaking of his love, every gesture and every breath had confirmed it utterly. His passion had been fierce, but his control always steady as a rock. What insanity had caused her to let him go?

When she did eventually break the silence, Hugh could sense her struggle. "Hugh — I am not remotely interested in the conference as such. Rather I realise I've been a fool, though it's taken so long for it to sink in. I only came back to Ireland because it would give me an opportunity to speak to you. The truth is that within weeks of being without you, I sensed that I had cut my own life line. I hadn't thought things out; I could not think. There were times, Hugh, when I tried to forget I ever met you; yet switching off like that was impossible. Above all, I was cruel to blame you for a tragedy that could have happened in a hundred different ways."

Barbara could not go on, and Hugh placed a tender hand on her shoulder, as her frame jerked with violent sobs. He eased her head towards his chest, and she listened in disbelief while he spoke.

"Barbara, I can understand how you feel. At the moment, both of us are still in the grieving process. If there was anything for me to forgive, I have truly forgiven. Perhaps you were hard on me, but I couldn't blame you."

She tried to interrupt, but Hugh continued in a calm voice. "The truth of the matter is that you don't really know your real motivations at this moment. I think for both our sakes we should think things over a little more. You know the wisdom of that as well as I do. Indeed we both recommend that to our patients..." In fact, Hugh had not detected a hint of Barbara's determination, conscious only of her intense sorrow. He knew that her loss of weight and colourless face betrayed an agonised mind, and he couldn't help but notice that the hair that once fell about her shoulders in a glorious cascade of abandonment was now severely cut, seeming to reflect the general tension she exuded. Her pain lay heavily on his heart, but he knew he must exercise extreme caution, for an emotional response could be disastrous both for her and for Vicky.

For her part Barbara did not know how she had arrived safely back at the Shelbourne Hotel that night. Clearly she must have driven at a reckless speed, as it was now only drawing towards midnight. Flinging herself fully clothed on the bed, she tried to reassemble recent events. It was futile, however, as she was totally unable to focus her attention. What's more, rage and envy overtook her whenever she thought of Vicky. That cosmetic girl could easily turn the head of any man, for she had such a striking figure, and those eyes could melt a stone. But then, Father James was a shrewd man, who held the opinion that this affair could not last. He had granted that Vicky was attractive (though he had never elaborated!), but had added that she was far too young and immature to form a lasting relationship with Hugh. Maybe he was right, Barbara thought, kicking off her shoes none too gently. She was exhausted in body and mind, but sleep did not take its steady hold. A horrid night threatened to devastate her, as she recalled the harrowed expression on Hugh's face the day she deserted him, how she had flung her suitcases into the boot of her car. Hugh had walked with her to the gate but she had brushed passed his open arms. "Jesus — it would be impossible for him to forgive me," Barbara concluded. "I left him then when he needed me most, and now that he has found love, wouldn't it be unthinkable to cause him further heartbreak? No — I must not mention Vicky's name to him!"

Yet when she looked in the mirror the following morning, Barbara saw a dishevelled woman trying to come to terms with hell. As she flung the hairbrush on the dressing-table, she reaffirmed that she would not mention Vicky to Hugh, but she was not going to give him up either without one hell of a try.

THAT next morning Vicky finished only half a slice of toasted bread, her tea untasted. The previous night's fitful sleep had done nothing to restore her spirits, and having to go to work today was proving a physical and psychological trauma. Having hoped work might afford her some moments of escape from her predicament, upon arriving there Vicky quickly saw she had hoped in vain, as the customary pleasant atmosphere only highlighted her misery. Having prepared her counter, she was distracted by laughter, then recognised the happy voice of Mrs Denton, her cosmetic buyer. This elegant "Lady of Cosmetics", as she was widely known, was dealing with a sales rep, and as usual it was hard to tell if the caller had succeeded or failed in securing an order, for Mrs Denton had the enviable knack of letting the sales-person feel that his mission was a success either way.

Vicky studied this elegant lady for a moment, thinking here was a woman who had conquered sorrow. After three years of happily married life, her husband had died, whereupon she had decided to go into the cosmetic field. With courage and patience Mrs Denton had retrieved much of her stolen happiness. Despite such desperate efforts to think positively, Vicky only shuddered at the mere thought of losing Hugh to Barbara, a fate worse than death. Nonetheless that dreaded possibility was now already lurking not far back in her consciousness. Suddenly a tap on the shoulder brought her back to her surroundings, as Sophie told her that Hugh was on the phone.

Hugh was a little taken aback at Vicky's quiet insistence on directing the conversation, as his reason for ringing was to enquire how she herself was. Instead Vicky showed great interest in the proceedings at the psychiatric conference. Putting that down to a little uneasiness on Vicky's part that Barbara had attended, he addressed all her questions, both spoken and unspoken. With great care he pressed her into stating how she was now feeling, and though her words were reassuring, she answered with the voice of one who was preoccupied.

Later, a visit to the cloakroom afforded her the opportunity of a little solitude and a chance to freshen up, a break she thought, which might help her re-channel the unrelenting stream of thoughts that was etching itself in her tormented mind. On her way back, she stopped to survey the fascinating display in the toy department, her weary train of thought once again rattling at full speed. Pausing, she placed her hand for a moment on the life-like fur of a huge teddy bear. This larger-than-life mascot called Bill stood sentinel over the children's wonderland, part of a permanent display. Vicky gazed at it intently, as did so many adults, not to mention astounded children, for its outstretched arms seemed to welcome the weary of all ages. The beady eyes behind their quaint spectacles were mysteriously alive, as if both chiding foolishness, yet still glistening with acceptance and comfort. How Vicky wished she could share her secret fears with wise old Bill. Half-believing, she looked up again at his crusty countenance, almost hearing him mutter that the refusal to make a decision was not a clever decision at all! But for the moment, duty called, so she headed back to her counter with a step that could not possibly keep pace with her thoughts.

The single cup of coffee in the downstairs Brown Thomas restaurant before leaving on her lunch-break did little to protect her from the cold wind that now crept in through every bush around St Stephen's Green. Many of the trees were now quite bare, others still clinging to clusters of winter leaves, as if reluctant to yield them to the sweeper's brush. Surveying the scene, she thought fondly of the old man who had interrupted her in her hell-bent task of mastering the secret wisdom of Freud and Jung. There was the very seat on which they sat. Beyond the pond itself rippled as prattling ducks glided in unison towards the far corner, where an old man was emptying the contents of a paper bag into the water. As the crusts and chunks of bread spilled out, the quacking grew louder, and the army of beggars around his feet increased in numbers. The man now folded the white bag neatly and placed it in the pocket of his heavy coat. As he reached down to retrieve his walking stick, Vicky suddenly recognised him. It definitely was him, the lonely man who had talked to her that day when she was trying to study. For a second she wondered should she talk to him, as if his advanced years might have given him a wisdom from which she could now benefit, though recalling their last chat, she highly doubted it! Besides, at this moment she would be scarcely able even to describe her predicament, as her monstrous dilemma had not yet unfolded all its threatening aspects even to herself. Vicky watched as he paused, looked up thoughtfully at the sky, withdrew a cap from his pocket and deftly tugged it onto his head with one hand, before hobbling away. Only then did she realise that the grayish cloud overhead had begun to shed an unpleasant drizzle.

Her afternoon stint at the Chanel counter was characterised by a mechanical lifelessness, until a florist courier was unexpectedly ushered by Sophie in Vicky's direction. Vicky's hands could hardly follow her mind's intent as they untied the message attached to a dozen roses, and she almost tore the little envelope together with its contents:

My Dearest Vicky, I am worried about you, and I do hope you are feeling better now as I cannot wait to see you tonight. One night of not being able to see you is like a week. Please think of each rose, Vicky, as a big kiss and hug. With all my love, to the one I love.

Forever thinking of you darling. Hugh

Yet for all their lovely sentiment, each word read like a cruel fish hook being savagely plucked from her heart.

THAT night the Abbey Tavern in Howth resounded with hand-clapping, foot stamping and spasmodic yahoos, signalling the time for a slow air, in this instance Mary Sheehan singing *Carrickfergus*. Hugh squeezed Vicky's hand and while she acknowledged the gesture, he realised her response lacked the intensity that usually characterised such tender moments. Studying her profile, he wondered was he imagining it or did he see the outward image of a tortured soul? Several times during the night he had noticed that Vicky had a far-away look. Had he been able to read her mind, of course, he would have understood immediately. Indeed Vicky's silence was killing her, as the precious secret of her pregnancy still remained a secret, leaving her in the throes of a cruel dilemma as she struggled with whether or not she could tell him. While the thought of Hugh being father to her child was a source of ecstasy, how could she expect good fortune if she prevented him reuniting with his wife, given that she found it tortuous to think of Barbara's pain? On the other hand, Hugh was now such a real part of her, part of her mind and body, that the very thought of losing him had become an unbearable agony.

Hugh had informed Vicky that Barbara would be coming for the conference, so that had been no secret, nor was he surprised that Vicky should show such interest in their meetings there. Over the evening she asked him if they had talked for long, what had they talked about, how long she would be staying in Dublin, where she was staying, and so on. Yet one question was all she truly wanted to know:

"How do you feel about her now, Hugh?"

By way of answering, Hugh drew Vicky close to him in a protective hug. The reply when it came was slow, but unrehearsed.

"Vicky, I loved Barbara — I've told you that. I now feel sorry for her, as she has aged greatly. When I look at her, I think of Karl, and when she looks at me she thinks of Karl too. I'd be a cheap liar to deny that if I could take away her pain, I would. But I cannot. Barbara was deeply wounded and made her decision, and I must respect that. You asked me earlier if there was someone in her life. No, there isn't. Still, I felt so sorry for her that I could not tell her how much I loved you — not yet, anyway," at which words Vicky winced.

"And what about your priest friend, Father James? Was he at the conference?"

"He was, darling. And I sure found it hard to keep serious when I thought of the name you gave him — I don't think he'd like being called Bones II. Poor old James has got a bit cranky in his old age, and very, very nosey."

Vicky so longed to tell Hugh what she really thought of the malicious cleric, but she remained silent.

There was no doubt in Hugh's mind over the next week that somehow a change had been wrought in the heart of his beloved Vicky. Their meetings lacked something, nor was it the normal cooling that transforms the heat of a new relationship into a more pragmatic accepting process. Finally one night he made a direct approach.

"Vicky darling, I can only hope and pray I haven't done something wrong. If I have, please, please tell me — I beg of you."

Vicky assured him that he hadn't, that he must be imagining things. The following night, still perturbed, he held Vicky in the gentle but firm manner of a parent trying to get the truth out of a child.

"Vicky, if you have met someone else, please tell me. It would be easier for the both of us," his eyes piercing and appealing.

If Hugh spent these nights in fitful sleep, Vicky hardly slept at all. Instead she spent endless hours recalling her mother's anguish when the bread-winner of their happy little family had walked out. Yet it was only after her mother had died that she could begin to make sense of the constant arguing and raised voices. Most of all Vicky remembered the visible pall of hurt that covered her mother's face whenever Vicky enquired about her father. And then had come the meeting with that father who had absented himself for ten years, only to find him a broken man.

One evening, Vicky studied some photos of her mother, selecting three for closer scrutiny. The first was taken prior to her marriage, Linda looking radiant. The second was the one which stood by her mother's bedside, the wedding photo. Here was the glorious bride whose every wish had been granted. The third showed Vicky with her mother on Confirmation Day, Vicky then eleven years of age, just a year after her father had left. The young girl in this photo was suitably preoccupied, but a closer look at her mother's face startled Vicky, in particular the distinctly dark circles under the eyes which had been nowhere visible in the earlier photos. A quick look at a few photos taken on later occasions confirmed that dramatic disimprovement. Replacing the photos, Vicky lay back on her bed, understanding the intensity of her mother's pain. She thought of Barbara, whose face also reflected evidence of a similar mental torture scored on human flesh. Her desertion of Hugh had been cruel beyond belief, but Vicky imagined her state of mind, her deed done in the throes of grief. Her demented rage had needed to find some outlet and Hugh was the obvious target. And how Barbara must feel now, Vicky thought, once more stretched upon the wrack. What's more, she had seemed not entirely without honour, having begged Vicky not to mention her pathetic approach in the hotel. As the doorbell rang, Vicky shuddered, accepting finally that she must face the most wretched task ever handed her.

For all his age and experience, Hugh was terrified when Vicky told him she had something difficult to say to him. Desperately trying to control his reaction, he quickly sat down, shifting Babycham without noticing her at all. He remembered reading that men who are condemned to death do not cry, rather collapse in a stupor of panic and fright, and he feared this might be happening to him.

Try as she might, Vicky could not look into his eyes as she finally spoke.

"Hugh, we must stop seeing each other. I should have told you some time ago, but I could not."

Stunned, Hugh managed to ask, "Vicky, is there someone else?"

"No, Hugh, its not that, it's..."

Cupping her two hands in his palms, Hugh took an unsteady breath and, after what seemed an age, finally spoke.

"It's the difference in our ages — I knew you were drifting from me, Vicky."

Nodding her head, Vicky buried her face in his chest. "Oh, Hugh, I don't know how to say it, but I have to tell the truth. While I feel just about able to bridge the two worlds we come from, I do not feel able for the years that also separate us..."

"I know we sorted out the gap between psychiatry and cosmetics," Hugh replied, "but I don't know any way to fix the gap between our ages."

"I'm so sorry, Hugh," Vicky sobbed, "but I've been so uncomfortable with this for so long."

"Christ, I always knew that this would come between us, that this was all too good to be true.

God, what I'd give to be able to roll back the years!"

His voice now fell into a whisper:

"Vicky, darling I'm going to miss you so much, you who are everything to me. Perhaps you might change your mind, indeed I beg of you to think it over. But I will not stand in the way of your happiness. And you have my untold thanks for the joy you have given to me."

Knowing it was impossible to utter any further words, Hugh stood torn, wondering should he wait and try to calm the almost hysterical Vicky, or would he serve her best by leaving? Unable for his own grief, he chose the latter course, and though the hall-door closed silently, it was five minutes before Vicky heard the Mercedes start. Dashing to the window, she was just in time to see it disappear into the open street, as her heartbroken cries rose even higher.

Two days later, Vicky sat at home reading and re-reading the letter she had just received.

...To be honest I find it difficult to write this. I myself have not recovered, but it is my greatest wish that you begin to come to terms with the parting of our ways. I'm deeply grateful that you agreed to keep the earrings and bracelet as a memento of our happy days — and what happy

*days they were. I thank you in particular for
Christmas night. For me too it was a special and
sacred experience.*

*Vicky, it would be selfish of me to try to hold
on to you. You're a beautiful girl with a most
delightful mind. I find it difficult to say what I
want to say — words are not enough, and
inspiration just isn't coming these days.*

*Look after yourself, Vicky. Your memory will
always live in my heart, but my greatest wish for
you now is that you will find happiness and love,
whatever path you follow. Hugh*

The letter, Vicky knew, was a gross under-
statement. Yet, whatever pain and grief they both
would suffer, Vicky tried to take some consolation
from picturing Hugh and his wife re-building their
life. Two weeks later, in tears, she related the news
of the tragic break-up and her secret pregnancy to
Brian in Johannesburg. Sobbing into the phone,
she explained she felt she must escape from a
Dublin haunted with such memories— for her
own sake, Hugh's, and that of her child. Always
the angel of mercy, Brian immediately understood
her plight and arranged everything. A week after,
he phoned her back to say that all was in order for
Vicky to leave for South Africa the following
month.

OVER those last weeks at work, Vicky took pains to explain that while Hugh was the kindest man she had ever met, she simply could not cope with his single-minded dedication to his profession and to his books. Despite her efforts, however, none of the girls at work were at all convinced. Fortunately for her, her last evening in Brown Thomas finally arrived, for the strain of living out a falsehood was draining her, never mind the acute pangs of sorrow that daily assaulted her, coupled with the unbearable pressure of keeping her pregnancy secret.

As Vicky served her last customer, the music stopped and the main lights simultaneously dimmed. Only the thin flourescents remained on, throwing a weird bluish shade over all, yet providing just enough light to illuminate the sheer grandeur of the store, from its sleeping chandeliers to its austere windows. A trickle of customers headed for the main door as the girls tidied their counters, and a till rattled here and there. Unobserved, Vicky looked about the magnificent store, regarding the various counters where she could almost hear the giggles and outright laughter of many happy encounters. She thought of the restaurant, picturing the exact position of the table where she had undertaken her first conversation with Hugh. At that a flood of memories overwhelmed her, and she turned to regard the very step from which she had tossed the psychology book in triumph, only to strike the outraged Mr Klein.

Shortly after she was joined by Louise, Sophie and Sharon, who read her sorrow instantly. Together they ushered her to Davy Byrne's, where a farewell drink was planned. Little did she know that twenty years would pass before the doors of Brown Thomas would again close behind her, as she walked towards the pub with a heavy step.

Vicky did her utmost to keep a brave face throughout the clinking of glasses, the loud chatter and the occasional goodbyes and hugs of the early leavers. Frank, the manager of Davy Byrne's, aided by his capable staff, entered the circle with a large iced cake and placed it on the table. Vicky had difficulty reading the inscription surrounded by several love-hearts, but when she could focus better, she realised that the blur was caused by her own tears, as she made out the message "We'll miss you, Vicky." Everyone felt permitted now to have a cry, and Vicky too availed of the opportunity. As the night wore on, the crowd thinned out. Sharon left, then Sophie's boyfriend arrived to collect her. Finally, it was Louise's turn to leave with her escort, and the pair walked Vicky to her car.

It was a wretched homecoming back at the bungalow, and Babycham was clearly puzzled at the sobbing figure lying fully clothed on the bed. Vicky looked once more in the direction of the phone, where minutes before, in a moment of absolute agony, she had rung Seagrave House just to hear Hugh's voice for the last time. Yet the phone had only rung and rung, and then to her horror, finally rung off.

THREE days later Vicky sat at her dressing table, totally overtaken by a terrifying feeling of loss. No cosmetics could obscure the fact that her lovely features were ravaged by inner torture. Wearily she leaned on her elbows and extended her fingers to cradle her head, the whiteness of her knuckles suggesting the interior whirlpool of her tortured thoughts and imaginings. Closing her eyes, she saw Hugh lift their new-born baby. How proud he looked! If it were a boy, how fitting that would be after the loss of Karl! On the other hand, he would make a super dad to a girl, watching her growing from a little girl into adolescence and young womanhood. She would adore him, Vicky thought, envisioning her asking him to drive her to her first dance, Hugh taunting her in a most outrageous fashion so that Vicky must intervene, while his laughter raises the roof. Father eventually walking his daughter to the car, one arm around her shoulder, while she skips alongside him. Then would come the time when she no longer wants Dad to escort her...

An unbelievable rage that had become a feature of these daily, interior monologues suddenly brought Vicky back to herself. Hugh's letter of farewell was within arm's reach, and she retrieved it once more to stare at its contents. By now she had studied every letter of every word hundreds of times, almost every twist and turn of the pen, noting that the writing lacked the carefree touch which had characterised his earlier notes, more like something written by a tired, arthritic hand.

Suddenly the sound of crackling paper and panicked breathing filled the little bedroom. Shaking uncontrollably, Vicky was scarcely conscious of her hand clenching in a painful, bruising convulsion. Like a drunken woman, she staggered back to the room she had left an hour before, her unfinished letter to Hugh lying on the table. With one savage swipe, she clutched the writing-pad, almost spraining her wrists in a bid to tear it in halves. Beyond control, she wrenched the car keys from the rack, slammed the front door and headed for her car. As she inserted the keys in the lock, they slipped from her twitching fingers. What's more, she had left the door unlocked again, the third or fourth time in the last few days.

In no time, she was on her way to Howth. It was as if her demented brain pressed that accelerator, causing many a placid driver to give way, and many a pedestrian to stop in his tracks. As she drove, she asked herself over and over again just why should she surrender her life to Barbara? Barbara who had her chance and blew it! What great madness had stopped her from telling Hugh about her pregnancy? Why in God's name should she let slip a lifetime of happiness with the man she would die for, to give it all away to that hard-hearted man hater!? What insanity had caused her to lie to Hugh, to spin such a ridiculous yarn about the difficulty she had with the difference in their ages? She laughed aloud, but it was more a hysterical release than any sound of joy. Indeed the drive to Howth was more like a journey hurtling down the rapids of a treacherous river. Slowing down on the last ascent of the coast road, she was perspiring freely as she drew her car to a halt outside Seagrave House. Yet that clammy perspiration shortly turned into cold sweat, as she spied a strange car at the gate. She reversed in panic, rear wheels skimming a jutting rock overlaid with grass. Continuing back for a hundred yards, she drew into the gateway of an adjacent field, where she discovered that by leaning forward a little in the driver's seat, she could command a perfect view of the front of Seagrave without her car being fully seen.

Suddenly she froze in shock, her greatest fear confirmed, as Hugh and Barbara walked towards the gate, Hugh opening it to allow Barbara through. They then walked side by side out of sight up the narrow road. Vicky gazed after them, like one in the throes of a heart attack. For several minutes the car itself shook as if in sympathy with its grief-stricken occupant. After a time its front wheels pulled to right angles, and the engine revved up to a pitch normally reached only on race tracks. The car then swung out recklessly and roared down the narrow road in the opposite direction to which Hugh and Barbara had taken.

Vicky's nerves suddenly snapped as she came to Sutton Cross where the unmerciful screech of brakes sounded from several cars as she sped through a red light. A Garda squad car did an immediate U-turn and raced after her at breakneck speed. When she stopped, two Gardai walked around her car while a third waited for her to roll down the window. Furious, he gradually settled down to the stern business of taking details of her tax and registration, though Vicky barely heard him telling her something about prosecution pending, and to produce her driving licence somewhere within fourteen days. Moreover, why did he persist in asking her if she were Okay? The Garda car followed her at some distance before eventually turning off up the Malahide Road. Having come to herself, a single thought now horrified her, namely, what if she and her baby had been killed outright?

In fact Barbara's visit that day to Seagrave needed no explanation. It was but one of many such visits, as Nora, Hugh's house-keeper, was at that moment complaining bitterly to a local shop assistant, speaking as if the middle-aged lady behind the counter were the one responsible. Indeed the vehemence of her harangue afforded her listener little chance of reply!

"I don't know what's got into that man. For one of them nerve doctors, you'd think he'd know better. That little Vicky girl — my God, she was gorgeous. None of that uppityness. She'd come into the kitchen, sit down, and chat like a Christian. She was like a breath of fresh air in that house. You'd know that he was sweet on 'er. Sure didn't she save him from goin' out of 'is mind? I know that they say it was the death of that young boy that made that Barbara one go away, but sure, my God she was always a bit daft — daft as a brush. An' didn't she leave him before? She used to give out to Dr Hugh for smokin' his pipe, and if he dragged in a bit o' muck on 'is boot she'd have a fit. An' you know yourself he's one of them outdoor men. You know what she says to me the other day? — make sure ye take the fat off the steak, says she 'cos Dr Hugh shouldn't eat any fat. Now I ask ye — an' me knowin' well that the poor man loved the fat o' the sirloin. Be God, little

Vicky never said a word like that to me. Ye see there was somethin' lovely about that girl. None o' that oul' nonsense. I'm tellin' ye, the man is goin' loopy. I know this much — if that Barbara one is comin' to stay, I won't be doin' the week-end cookin 'an' washin'. I thought it was only men like my Jack that went a bit funny. They must all be the bloody same; God love her, that little Vicky will be broken hearted. She even showed me the book she got 'im for Christmas. The poor ting t'ought she'd never wait to give it to 'im. An' if ye saw the lovely card she sent to t'ank me for cookin' at Christmas! I'm tellin' ye now, the man is losin' the bit 'e has. An' ye know what — that Barbara one has even stayed over a few nights. She's tryin' to put her charm on the misfortunate man. I says a prayer for 'im every mornin', that 'e'll see sense."

Apart from the occasion of Karl's death, there was no worse time in Hugh's life than the period spanning the writing of that final letter of farewell to Vicky and his own departure to America. These were days of weariness and nights of wakefulness, in which every iota of mental energy seemed stalled on a treadmill, unable to help him to arrive at a decision. Recurring doubts were now like white-hot knives twisting in the wounds of his unspeakable loss. If Barbara was unaware of Vicky's decision, she was all the same a keen student of the human mind. To try to convince Hugh that he was wasting his life on the younger woman could be a tricky business. Clever as she was, she did not know that every time she exerted pressure on Hugh, she leaned on a festering wound. Still, she was curious to know why it was so easy to see Hugh almost any evening she chose. Perhaps the tide was turning in her favour?

Accepting that he finally had to face his dilemma, Hugh still did not really fathom the reason why he had chosen to walk down Grafton Street that day. "Even if I'm in denial," he thought, his heart racing, "what harm is there in taking a discreet look?" And so he stopped at the window of Brown Thomas, where he had long since learned the exact spot from which he could view Vicky unnoticed. However this time his features froze in shock, for she was not there, and another girl served at the Chanel counter. For years after he could never say from where he had summoned the strength to walk on. Small wonder that he had irritated shoppers by his slow, leaden steps. "If he's short-sighted," grumbled one woman in a hurry, "well then he should have a white stick!"

In truth, however, his eyes had ceased to function, having turned inward to a series of memories now set in motion: — the restaurant in Brown Thomas, the broken-hearted girl he had comforted at the breakfast table; Killakee House Restaurant where he had heard her laughter echo over the Dublin hills, had seen her eyes burst into blazing stars as the huge bouquet was wheeled in. He saw her dash again from the counter on Christmas Eve and fling herself into his arms as would a child. By the time he reached the carpark, he felt a part of him had died. Yet, driving back to Seagrave, he also felt the tiniest twinge of guilt at having returned to the shop. It was not the manful thing to do, and had Vicky been there, he could have her caused further sickening heartache. Nor did he know how he would survive the following days.

Meanwhile, Barbara's womanly intuition told her that Hugh was nearing decision-time. Moreover she felt that things were running in her favour, for he seldom went out, and spent most of his time simply reflecting. Still Barbara failed to see that so many hours of deep thought were also accompanied by a suicidal sense of loss. For Hugh, his choice was simple in logical terms, but reason alone could not drag him from this emotional quicksand. One thing was sure, however; he could not remain living in Seagrave House. Everything in its vicinity invited memories of tragic sorrow, Karl's death, Barbara's several desertions, and now the loss of Vicky. "How she loved being here," he thought. "She gave her heart to every breeze that wafted over Howth, to every wave that washed its shore — she also gave herself, heart and body, to me....O God — help me to think — to make some sense." Defeated, he tried to concentrate on Barbara's well-being. Certainly she seemed to have changed, and there was nothing she wouldn't do for him these days.

THAT'S the grave of the young lad who was killed." The two grave diggers had paused in their labour and were looking towards a grave several yards away. They saw a tall man placing a fresh bouquet, standing it upright against the plinth. Then, in a most curious fashion he sat, shoulder against the headstone and both feet straddling the neat rail that surrounded the grave. It was Dr Hugh. The grave diggers thought it strange, not least on a chilly afternoon.

"He'll never get over it," whispered one of the men. "It's like as if he thinks he's talking to the little chap."

Which was exactly what Hugh was doing — a deeply silent spiritual communion with his son. He didn't have to think of words either, even though his heartfelt feelings ran differently to the pattern of many of his previous visits. And never before had he sat like this, risking his reputation as a psychiatrist. Still Hugh did not care, as if he knew it was to be the last of these father-and-son, heart-to-heart chats.

He found himself telling Karl that his heart was torn asunder, explaining that Barbara really had loved their little boy, and that she was perfectly right not to agree to that bike, which had proved the cause of this entire wretched nightmare. He told Karl how his heart had yearned for love as Barbara had not been there to comfort him, though she did not really mean to cause such sadness by her leaving. Hugh continued in this wordless discourse for some time before he came to Vicky. He begged Karl to ask God to send her happiness, confessing to his son that he loved Vicky more than all the lovers on this earth had ever loved, but that their love was just not to be.

The nearer of the two grave diggers then observed Hugh press a white handkerchief over his face, covering his eyes in it. He studied the silent grief of the mourner for almost ten minutes, until finally Hugh used the grave stone to draw himself into an upright position. As he staggered backwards, both grave diggers made as if to rush to his assistance, then withdrew as he steadied himself. They pretended to have seen nothing, respecting his privacy, yet they did draw nearer, aware that more than one mourner had taken a turn at the grave of a loved one. One last time, Hugh touched the bouquet that he had placed there, deciding to lay it flat lest the wind should dislodge it. Then, clasping the gravestone, he spoke as if he were holding little Karl, just loudly enough for the grave diggers to distinctly hear the hoarse, tearful voice utter, "Wish me luck, son — wish me luck."

Hugh turned reluctantly and walked slowly towards the entrance of the cemetery. He turned back once, paused for a minute, then went on towards his car. The grave diggers, hardened as they were to such scenes, were deeply moved. "He'll never get over it," said one of them again.

"Funny," said the other, "the Missis never seems to come with him."

"No," his mate replied. "Sure, didn't she leave him when the grave was still fresh, and even that was the second time, someone told me. Still, she's back now. I saw him one night in the Abbey Tavern with a real smasher. He's supposed to be a psychiatrist, but by all accounts he let her slip through his fingers. He's not using the head too well, poor man."

The following day a Boeing 707 climbed smoothly from Dublin Airport, and after a few minutes of north-bound flight turned westerly. Barbara pretended to look past Hugh as if to watch the clouds float along outside the plane. In fact, she was studying his profile. He was still gazing with misty eyes over towards Howth, and his throat seemed to tighten. "He's bound to be upset," she thought, and placed her hand on his. With that

Hugh smiled bravely and acknowledged her touch.

A week later Vicky walked wearily to her car on St Stephen's Green, after some last minute shopping. A tall, gaunt, pale figure broke ranks with the other busy pedestrians, and walked towards Vicky, his Roman collar now visible. It was Father James and his first words almost knocked Vicky to the pavement. "Hugh has gone back to America with Barbara, his wife," he said, speaking as if the universal church had resolved an enormous moral problem, with himself as the lynch-pin in its solution. With the scolding manner of a preacher trying to convert a reluctant sinner, he went on:

"It is as it should be, my dear, — they are meant for each other. What's more, Seagrave House is sold." As he took a breath mint, Vicky noted that he had not even addressed her by name, and she felt again the ice-cold glare that she had experienced on Christmas morning. Turning, she walked away, fearing she might otherwise strike him.

If Vicky thought nothing could hurt any more, the process of selling her and Linda's bungalow proved her numbness was not complete. Leaving Babycham in the care of a kind neighbour similarly cut her to the quick, her feeling of betrayal intolerable, as the little creature purred and clung to her cardigan.

FOR Hugh, Florida proved a pleasant place, as the weather was heavenly, with lots of sunshine. It was a good spot for psychiatric practice, since many people were now acquiring their personal analyst. Hugh in particular was very much on call, and Barbara had her own consulting rooms. Yet after a while Hugh decided to accept a post as lecturer, which afforded him more time to spend at home.

The first year of their reunion started well, as Hugh made an all-out effort to make Barbara happy. Several times he urged her that she need not work at all — his salary was more than sufficient. What's more, time off in Florida was precious. Even if one did not enjoy the active life, there was always the opportunity to drape oneself under the sun, perhaps at the edge of a swimming pool, or on one of the golden beaches. Yet if Barbara chose the busy indoor life of work and study, Hugh preferred a balanced diet of work and play. He was an excellent swimmer, an accomplished sailor and a competent horseman. Their different life-styles caused some tension but overall was manageable. A day of completely different activities for both often ended with an exotic evening meal.

This routine was not always the case, however, and in the second year of their new life together it became more of a rare pleasure. Moreover Barbara was aware of a change in Hugh. He remained faithful and gentle, but he did not laugh much any more. If he pretended to be amused, she sensed that he did so for her sake. That Hugh was somewhat reticent had always been part of his attractiveness, but there was no explaining this. He was behaving much as he did after Karl's death. She was becoming weary of his long silences, and one night she asked out straight if he missed Vicky, as there was certainly no other woman in his life. He replied that he did not, but Barbara could never forget the piercing darkness of eyes that lied.

Shortly after, Barbara took advantage of a quite afternoon to write to her mother. She voiced her increasing disquiet, "...I know why he called the new boat *Sea Scamp*. He admitted that he taught Victoria how to sail in our boat back in Howth, but maybe I'm just a bit touchy! Still, I told you our dog Trooper was killed on the highway. We decided that dogs are too troublesome, and decided to get a cat. That was fine — but guess what he wants to call the new kitten? — Babycham. It didn't take much detective work to establish where he got that name from!" Indeed

Barbara's mother rightly suspected the beginnings of more serious problems.

One evening Barbara was searching Hugh's bookshelves for a reference book. What was this volume on Irish Antiquities doing in his psychology section? She opened it, and looked aghast at the neat writing inside the cover: *To my darling Hugh, wishing you a really Happy Christmas 1974. XXXX I love you so much. Your own Vicky*

This unhappy discovery was the bench-mark against which Barbara measured many subsequent happenings. Meanwhile Hugh continued to sit up into the small hours, even though Barbara had other designs on how this precious time might be spent!

His compliments on Barbara's dress began to ring hollow, and when they discussed cases, he always managed to talk about the problem of the older man and the younger woman. Barbara sensed the deep emotion that always accompanied his comments. Occasionally the artificial shell he had built around many of his truer feelings just was not strong enough. One evening when Barbara and Hugh went horse-riding, Barbara did a few trial runs to impress Hugh. Yet all Hugh could see was Vicky again, her long hair flying, only to be awakened from his memories by a shout of "Bloody pig," and a sharp crack. If the horse was frightened, it was nothing to the shock Barbara experienced when Hugh drew alongside her, snatched the whip from her, flung it into the trees, and hissed at her, "That is totally unnecessary!"

Barbara withered, as she could almost feel hatred in that voice.

They went to a party a few nights after, a kind of informal affair. Barbara was carrying on in a rather loud voice, and one look at her could tell that she was pretty high. For quite a while her voice predominated, then there was a call for silence, as Barbara was going to sing. She began, "Fish, gotta sing — and birds gotta fly — I'm gonna love one man till I die — Can't help lovin..."

Her voice breaking, she began to choke back tears. Knowing it was futile, she collapsed into an armchair, fists beating its sides. The on-lookers knew immediately that something serious was amiss, and several pairs of eyes sought out Hugh. That evening brought home all too clearly to her that she laboured in vain. Soon after Barbara moved out, eventually moving on to Canada, where her meeting a doctor in Montreal drew her on a tide away from Hugh's world.

Two months after she left, Hugh was glancing at the morning mail, when one letter caught his attention. It was stamped "Return to Sender" and had been re-addressed by the post office to Barbara Whittaker c/o Hugh's address in Florida. Hugh stared in disbelief at its original destination: Victoria Vaughan, c/o Brown Thomas, Grafton Street, Dublin.

He felt compelled to read its contents, and perspired freely as its message seemed to mock him:

Dear Victoria, By the time you receive this letter, I will have left for Canada. I feel I owe it to you to contact you, as you were very forthright with me. I don't know what your present situation is, nor would I be surprised if you have been maintaining contact with Hugh unknown to me. Anyway, for the record, I owe it to you to let you know that our attempt at reconciliation has not worked out. After you kindly stood down, things never really improved. In fact they worsened. I do not blame anybody, Victoria, but the fact of the matter is that even first time round I never really felt I possessed Hugh. You may not know that I left him briefly, before Karl's death, as I don't think I told you. I never thought that Hugh and yourself would ever make a go of things because of your age difference. Obviously I misjudged. You should know, Victoria, that he has pined for you from the very beginning. I've watched him so often with a smile that could not hide his pain.

I do not wish to upset you by letting you know this, Victoria. What you decide is entirely up to you. I just felt it was fair to fill you in. Thanks again for your understanding. Yours very sincerely, Barbara Whittaker

In fact Barbara had hoped for Hugh's sake that he would contact Vicky and bring her to Florida. She did not realise however, that Father James had been in contact with Hugh, informing him of Vicky's departure to South Africa, having ferreted this information out of Brown Thomas. Hugh had answered Father James' letter, and emphasised that he wanted to know even just the city she had gone to. He told Father James in subsequent letters that he was infuriated by the fact that Father James stubbornly avoided all mention of Vicky in spite of Hugh's insistence. A fortnight after reading Barbara's letter to Vicky, however, Hugh received a letter with handwriting he did not recognise. The notepaper bore the crest of the order to which Father James belonged. It was the announcement of the death of Hugh's friend.

Over several weeks Hugh battled with a horrendously powerful urge to return to Dublin and begin a relentless search for Vicky. While his mind told him that by now she would have picked up the pieces and started a new life with someone else, his heart screamed otherwise. For Vicky's sake, though, he summoned every ounce of courage and desisted.

ONCE again Hugh spent long evenings studying and preparing lectures. His dedication to his profession was the only source of energy or interest, though he tried to revive his love for music, with limited success. His first Christmas Eve alone in the sunny villa almost drove him suicidal, as he could never forget that white Christmas at Seagrave. Every detail of it: Vicky's excitement, the Christmas tree, the log fire, Christmas dinner, and most of all that unforgettable Christmas night, was as clear as if it happened yesterday. Over and over again he played one track of the LP Vicky had bought him, *Carrickfergus*, which whisked him back to nights of overwhelming happiness.

Subsequent Christmas times were not the only stimuli that triggered fond memories. How often in the years following had he gazed out at night towards the hill south of the villa and seen the sea of lights that bordered the ocean. He thought always of the night lights of Dublin and waited in vain for the echoes of laughter that one night rang round Killakee House when Vicky made her awful confession and he made his. Then came the poignant moment when he reached for that volume comparing the work of Freud and Jung.

The book was slightly out of his reach, and when it toppled down on his study desk, out flew the little well-pressed blue flower. He had removed it from his diary on a black night the year before when he had drunk a little too much, and afterwards he could not recollect where he had put it.

One Sunday in the late 1980s, Hugh sat in his sitting room, watching the film of South Pacific on the TV. When it came to that beautiful song, *This Nearly was Mine*, the words virtually tore open the scars upon his heart: "This nearly was mine — one hope to be living for — now I'm alone, one dreaming of paradise — into my heart she came, only to fly away — now, now, I'm alone."

He reached into his pocket and opened a small black jewel box. Tears gathered and fell upon the ring it contained, the engagement ring he had hoped to put on Vicky's finger. In fact he had carried the box bearing the inscription "To my darling Vicky, 1974," with him for nearly fifteen years now.

If Hugh had so often helped people in their bereavement, explaining to them patiently the six stages that precede recovery: denial, anger, bargaining, depression and finally, acceptance, he himself had only negotiated the first five steps with tortuous persistence. Having never reached the sixth phase, he remained very much the wounded healer.

EVEN if Vicky could not entirely forgive the twists and turns of fate that had led her to live in South Africa, she was delighted upon the birth of a healthy baby boy, Andrew, six months after she arrived. What's more, the years passed quickly enough as she settled into Brian's spacious home in Johannesburg, which she and Andrew shared with him. It was a well appointed residence, surrounded by a generous expanse of green lawn and swimming pool, and was situated in an exclusive area which had plenty of parkland round about.

Without a doubt Brian had showed his true colours. To Vicky he was a dear, dear friend and confidante, and most importantly he was like a father to her now growing son Andrew. When Andrew had reached school-going age, Vicky had taken a position as receptionist in the nearby Carlton Hotel. She knew she would have to provide for Andrew's fees at the Daleside College, a leading educational establishment run by the Salesian Fathers, where she hoped to send him after his early schooling.

For his part, Brian was concerned over these years that Vicky should try to get out a little. He organised barbecues, but Vicky seemed to be more engrossed in grilling chicken than in mixing with the company. The pubs in Johannesburg never interested her; they were entirely different from the likes of Davy Byrne's. Still she accompanied Brian on a few occasions each year to the theatre, and indeed only that seemed to take her out of herself.

As it happened, romance never really took a hold of Vicky, although Brian had introduced her to a colleague of his, a tall, attractive Irishman called Darren, and for two years they had gone out on a regular rota of dates. Vicky would never forget the birthday she had celebrated with Darren. She took great care getting ready, so much so that even Andrew teased her about it, Andrew who was never to know the pain his mother experienced as she selected a pair of earrings. She regarded the sapphire pair in the mirror, thinking of how she looked on her twenty-first birthday with Hugh. She could see his adoring glance, his rogueish smile as the massive bouquet was wheeled into the restaurant. Ultimately it was too much, and she replaced them sadly in their case.

On a Sunday afternoon shortly after, Darren and Brian sat down to a cold beer, and a perplexed Darren spoke.

"Brian, she's fabulous. She's everything a man could want in a woman, but she gives me the impression that she is afraid of becoming involved. I've given her every opportunity; I've asked her face to face would she marry me, but she has that cursed knack of giving a reply which is not a reply, if you know what I mean — and making you feel good about it! I just don't know what the hell to do."

Brian's reply was delayed, not to mention reluctant. "Darren, I told you before about Hugh. What's more, I know from speaking to Vicky that she sees everything of Hugh in Andrew. She's told me it's as though by having Andrew she still has Hugh. I've known Vicky for years, Darren, and I know her well enough to realise that she never really got over Hugh. My belief is that Vicky's heart is still back in Ireland."

And how true that was in so many ways! For example, Vicky had attended art classes where she had discovered she had quite a talent for painting. Some of her work was even exhibited locally, and many of her paintings were of the Irish countryside. Those of Killakee and Howth Head from several aspects were particularly striking, and even her teacher marvelled at the magical, yet melancholy atmosphere she created by her use of grey sky and gathering rain clouds.

As it happened, Andrew had indeed grown into a replica of Hugh, and Vicky was justly proud of him. From the start, he showed an extraordinary academic talent, excelling in maths and science. What's more, as he entered the realm of manhood, his tall athletic frame attracted a host of female admirers. Numerous medals and trophies for rugby union, tennis and athletics adorned a china cabinet, but he never ever referred to them except when asked, having inherited Hugh's casual modesty. The bond between Andrew and Vicky was powerful and profoundly healthy. Some years earlier he had asked Vicky about the events that led to his being born in South Africa, and she had given him a full and honest answer, such that Andrew had gained a deep appreciation of the sacrifices Vicky had made for him. However, his interest in Ireland was constantly reflected in his questioning, and Vicky loved the long, cosy chats with him. Just like Hugh, he adored the old tales of fairies and leprechauns, and Vicky often compared his kindness to that of Hugh. Indeed she had never stopped thinking of Hugh, sometimes wondering if he was still alive, was his wife good to him, was there a family? And such musings were always charged with a sadness and a longing!

HUGH eventually ceased to see any clients at all and concentrated fully on lecturing. His students, ready to detect an oddity in any lecturer, noted that Hugh's lectures always managed to contain reference to the Emerald Isle, and they consequently nicknamed him the "Irish Psyche".

Early in his fourth year of lecturing, however, Hugh became aware of a daily, nagging tiredness. His quick wit and deft turn of phrase were less and less in evidence, and his students noted that he was getting ever more irritable. His fatigue seemed to be especially acute in the morning, as if he had enjoyed only an hour or two's sleep, whereas in fact he rarely had less than six or seven hours. His appetite had also diminished considerably, yet he put it all down to depression. Being something of an expert in this field, he was quite convinced he would come through it, that he would work through it step by step. After all, it was normal that the mind would eventually react to such a traumatic succession of years.

Then, one morning when he had arisen particularly tired, he fell asleep and veered off the centre lane driving to work. A blast of a car horn caused him to panic, as his car glanced off the side of another car to his right. The other terrified driver was sufficiently in control to minimise the impact by evasive action, but Hugh felt a heavier impact on the rear of his own car, then a second one, as screeching brakes sounded far back along the highway.

Though he had sustained a minor whiplash injury, a broken wrist, and a bruised head, thankfully the seat-belt had prevented much more serious injuries. Still, lying in a restrained position in a hospital bed for two weeks proved to be very irksome. Accordingly Hugh was pleased when the specialist finally signalled an "all clear" that would allow him to re-enter the mainstream of his life. Though he faced a charge of dangerous driving, his conscience was clear, and he knew he could cope with that.

Still, to his dismay, the specialist harped on and on about Hugh's tiredness, as if oblivious to the fact that after all Hugh was quite knowledgeable himself in matters of physical as well as mental health. Still Hugh ultimately relented, and agreed to undergo a battery of tests suggested by the specialist.

The tests proved tedious and time-consuming, and the specialist treated Hugh at times with a distant, professional coldness that appalled him. Questions were not welcomed, and if Hugh pressed for an answer, only the bare minimum of information was forth-coming.

When the specialist finally scheduled an appointment to go over the results of his tests, Hugh discovered a part of his psyche of which he had been quite unaware. If the previous days of waiting had been tortuous by reason of the anger and impatience that possessed him, now that the moment of truth was imminent, Hugh was entirely overtaken by a paralysing fear. What if he were to be told he had cancer? What if he were to be condemned to a term of constant treatment which would drain him even further? Suddenly Hugh found himself contemplating the ultimate questions that confront a patient, even a medical professional, in such straits. What was dying like? Was there a life hereafter? Against the background of terror he glimpsed three figures. There was some consolation that he might see Karl again, but it quickly escaped from his confused thoughts. He then thought of Barbara, who had written him saying she would make her way to see him, though Hugh was indifferent about any such visit. Then, just as he focussed on an image of his beloved Vicky, Hugh had reason to wonder were he going insane. As it happened, he hadn't heard the nurse entering his room, who was now adjusting the blinds. Morning sunshine rushed through the window, as Hugh gazed in amazement at the silhouette of a lovely young female, who greeted him, "Good morning, Doctor Burke," in a distinctly Irish accent .

Hugh was barely able to reply. If he knew it was not Vicky, he still wished that even the illusion would last. The young nurse sensed he was perturbed, for Hugh could not hide it, becoming even more visibly upset as he asked her what part of Ireland she came from. A Dubliner, she listened with concern as he spoke of Howth, Seagrave House, the Abbey Tavern, and the Dublin mountains. It was the intensity of his speech that most struck her, and this young nurse quickly sensed that her presence had triggered something more in her patient than just fond memories of Dublin alone. It seemed, as she gazed into those deep haunted eyes, that as Hugh spoke of the places, a silent voice within him also spoke of a far more precious association with those locales. As he lay back, she watched tears fill his eyes, and Hugh was embarrassed as she offered him a tissue. Torn between a desire to find out what troubled him so deeply, and her professional duty not to become involved in a patient's private life, she felt to her astonishment Hugh take her hand. Nor did she resist as he squeezed it gently, sensing it was simply his way of telling her not to be concerned.

That afternoon the moment he had dreaded finally arrived. The specialist seated in front of him looked grave and aloof as always. As he spoke, Hugh unconsciously gripped the edge of the desk which separated them. However, upon hearing "The news is not too bad, Doctor," Hugh released his grip. "Basically, you have an acute anaemic condition," the doctor continued, "which can be treated. However, I am quite amazed that a man of your experience could have allowed this condition to develop so far. Obviously you must have been aware of a decline for a long time. It seems you have been extremely careless regarding your general health..."

Suddenly Hugh, in a totally unconscious manner, rose and left the specialist sifting through papers and still talking. In a matter of minutes he was packing his suitcase, hoping that perhaps a long walk in the open air would enable him to make sense of where his life was heading. Both his confusion and fond memories were pulling him in unknown directions, and he felt like a rudderless boat. Indeed, for all his years in medicine, it appeared the brilliant psychiatrist was still learning of the storm clouds that can bedevil the human mind.

GIVEN that the streets of Johannesburg perpetually teemed with humanity, Vicky was pleased that Bluebell's restaurant lay only a short distance away. Walking along, she reflected with amusement on how another strange twist of fate was now directing her towards this particular rendezvous. On the previous day Vicky had been shopping, the stores thronged with customers. Scanning a colourful display of fruit, she had felt a finger poking her ribs and a voice speaking into her disbelieving ear, "Now don't jump into the water, Vicky, unless you're able to swim!" Moreover, the speaker was mimicking perfectly the accent of Sister Joseph, the nemesis of Vicky's secondary school years! Oblivious of the impatience of busy shoppers and check-out girls, Vicky turned and threw her arms around Aisling Byrne, her best schoolfriend. Though they had not met for over twenty years, mutual recognition was immediate. As it turned out, Aisling had come to South Africa for her sister's wedding; still, the chances of two people meeting in a huge city, Vicky knew, must be one in a million. After having been separated for so many years by thousands of miles, both women sensed reminiscing was going to be wonderful!

As it was, Vicky remembered vividly the day Aisling left school, one year before sitting the leaving certificate. At first Aisling had been thinking only of the excitement of living in Philadelphia, where her father was being transferred on promotion from the Dublin branch of a multinational company. However, as time for leaving drew nearer, Aisling had begun to realise the harsher reality of leaving her best friend, and when the day finally arrived, both girls were in floods of tears.

Vicky also clearly remembered her next Monday morning at school, looking at Aisling's vacant bench. Sister Joseph however had no time for such sentiment, and immediately arranged for the bench to be removed from the classroom to make more space. While it was being carried out, the nun admonished Vicky, "Now that the other half of your adventurous duo has gone, perhaps you will at last settle down to some solid work, and shake the nonsense out of that giddy head of yours!"

In any case, lunch at Bluebell's was the perfect setting for a re-union. "I could not sleep last night, Aisling," Vicky cried, "as I looked forward so much to meeting you."

"Nor I," replied Aisling, who had also tossed and turned, wondering had their encountering each other been only in her imagination? "I mean, our lives have us living on opposite sides of the world; then, as if by a sheer miracle, I see you in the store. It's just too much to take in."

While Aisling could not wait to hear of the events that led to Vicky's living in such a great city, she was saddened to hear of Vicky's misfortune. Still, she found it impossible to refrain from raising the "older man" issue which had earlier seemed to bedevil a very romantic schoolgirl Vicky. Laughing, Aisling reminded Vicky of at least two occasions when she had been severely berated for being seen in the company of an older boy from a local school. Indeed it had been Sister Joseph's intention to inspire disgust and horror at the very idea of a school girl "keeping company", but flustered, the nun had unwittingly emphasised the age difference, describing the lad as if he had been old enough to be Vicky's father! While Vicky blushed furiously, one by one the other girls were overtaken by helpless laughter. The good Sister enjoyed the merriment, totally unaware of the fact that the laughter was at her own expense.

Several glasses each of South African wine helped revive further memories of many such school-day exploits. Vicky remembered vividly the day she was upbraided for inviting her companions to share sprays of her Estée Lauder. The lecture culminated in a stern warning that she could end up like the vain woman who gazed into the mirror and saw the devil. Then there was the time when Reverend Mother gave a talk on vocations. Taken unaware, the girls were asked one by one which career they would like to follow. When Vicky replied that she would like to be a beautician, Reverend Mother almost choked. There was a stunned silence as she stared in contempt at Vicky. Recovering, she could manage only one word, "Nonsense!" before going on to the next girl, Rachel, who replied that she would like to be a nun. If Reverend Mother was pleased indeed, the girls were shocked beyond belief, for Rachel was a tear-away who smoked in the toilets, bullied her classmates, and by the tender age of thirteen years had already become expert at attracting the attentions of the boys. Now, however, Sister Joseph softened her attitude towards the delinquent. This turnabout was a triumph indeed, and Rachel thoroughly enjoyed her new found favour, as no one would dare give the game away. Needless to say, the cloisters never did resound to the sweet voice of her chanting!

Aisling meanwhile also had her own history of misdemeanours. One day she had told Sister Joseph she had forgotten her homework. Instructed to empty her school bag, Aisling turned as red as a beet root. As she hesitated, Sister Joseph opened the bag and scattered the contents on the desk, only to stand like one afflicted by a vision of Hell itself. Employing the nails of forefinger and thumb like a forceps, she lifted a tattered copy of *The News of the World* from the pile of schoolbooks. In the ensuing tirade, Sister Joseph made Aisling repeat her name several times. "Do you know, girl, the meaning of that beautiful name?"

"It means 'dream or vision,' Sister," a trembling Aisling replied.

"Well, let me tell you, my girl, you're no vision and you're no dream. Instead you're more of a horrific nightmare!"

As they lingered over lunch, Vicky recalled Aisling's fascination with men in uniform, not least the time the object of her admiration was none other than a young priest! Whenever he visited the school to instruct the classes in all aspects of Catholic doctrine, Aisling's attention was not altogether rivetted on the lofty words of spiritual counsel delivered by the diligent curate.

Rather she was besotted and did not know why. Aisling's mother was herself intrigued by her daughter's sudden enthusiasm for early morning Mass in the convent, a practice then common among very few of her classmates. This infatuation did not go unnoticed either by Sister Joseph, who often sat in during these classes, and always led the girls in prayer prior to each visit of the priest. On one such occasion, the young priest was interrupted mid-way by a gasp of horror from the troubled nun whose gaze was fixed on Aisling's skirt. By dint of tugging and twisting in her seat, Aisling had accidently raised her hem-line above her knees. With fumbling fingers she now tried frantically to restore the skirt to its proper length, only this was not to be! As a punishment, she was seated during the next visit in the front row with a gaberdine draped over her knees. Her humiliation was salutary indeed, and after this incident, Aisling could not bear the priest even looking at her. Meanwhile her mother only noticed that Aisling suddenly preferred to sleep on instead of attending early morning worship.

Still, contrary to the expectations of her teachers, Aisling had done very well, and was now employed as an assistant manager in a leading Dublin bank. That she lived with a married man who was separated from his wife suggested, however, that perhaps her spiritual mentors were not altogether off-target in their prognosis!

Both Aisling and Vicky were reluctant to part as it neared the end of their lunch. Quite clearly a precious period of friendship and laughter had been retrieved, a friendship that would have certainly remained buried by the ever increasing span of years, had Aisling not spotted Vicky in the store.

Finally it was Aisling who spoke. "Vicky, you'll have to come to Dublin for a holiday — and I mean soon. You know how quickly time flies. Make up your mind now, within the next few weeks — maybe during the summer. You deserve a break."

At first Vicky did not speak. "You know I'd love to spend a holiday with you, Aisling," she finally replied. "It would be great, but...I don't think I could face the memories. It would be too much, I'm afraid, though I suppose deep down I must make one final trip to Dublin before I die, or my life somehow won't be complete."

"Nonsense Vicky! Let me hear no more of your not coming back to visit soon." And taking her diary from her bag, Aisling wrote her address on a blank page, tore it out, and pressed it into Vicky's hand.

TWO weeks later, Brian wondered how he would break the news to Vicky, who was only aware there were some problems in his bank. If redundancies were being sought, takers were few and far between. While Brian had given many years of faithful and distinguished service, for reasons that only the banking fraternity understood, it was precisely those of his vintage and performance that were being targeted. Only yesterday he had been offered a most tempting settlement, comprising a handsome lump-sum and a very respectable pension for life. Other attractive incentives were included, but the double-edged offer gave him just two weeks to decide. Still, this was an offer he could not refuse, and failure to reply in time would mean a total review of the offer and the possibility of a transfer. The deciding factor, however, was his overwhelming desire to return to Ireland, which this offer would surely allow at an opportune time under perfect circumstances. In short, Brian knew he would have to accept, yet he hated having even to discuss the matter with Vicky and Andrew. That very day, however, fate was to intervene once more!

As it happened, Andrew's academic achievements had won him distinction in Daleside

College, where the Salesians had given him every encouragement. And while Andrew had determined that medicine was going to be his career, he had also developed an insatiable interest in Ireland. One priest in particular had nurtured this preoccupation by supplying books of Irish interest. At home also, Andrew still wondered why his mother's eyes filled up whenever he showed her a book of Irish ballads, not knowing that Vicky always thought of happier days as she invariably found *Carrickfergus* included therein. Composing herself, she often sang a little of it for Andrew. "She sings it so softly — so sadly," her son always noted, perhaps somewhere in his subconscious remembering his mother lulling him to sleep with that same old Irish tune.

When the letter finally arrived, Andrew's heart soared at the sight of the Irish stamps. With trembling hands, he read the short but official looking message. Jumping up, he threw the letter into the air and hollered to Vicky, who was lying down in her room. In fact, she had already guessed from his excitement that the reply to Andrew's application to the renowned Royal College of Surgeons in Dublin had arrived. Stifling her true feelings, she embraced her ecstatic son. She smiled bravely, but Andrew sensed something in her reaction, and he decided not to mention the matter again that day. Instead shortly afterwards he phoned Brian and confided that he was worried about his mother being lonely once he left to study in Ireland. Unable to believe his ears, Brian immediately called Vicky and telling her about the redundancy he had been offered from his bank, he proposed that the three of them should return together to Ireland. Although Vicky greatly feared the re-awakening of painful memories, she could not deny some excitement at the prospect of returning to Ireland. At least her heart would not be torn by a separation from Andrew, nor by the loss of a dear, dear friend.

Two months later a taxi carried the three of them along the busy highway that led from Dublin Airport to city centre. Seated in the back with Andrew, Vicky was conscious only of a tremendous sense of change. Traffic seemed to have trebled, and new housing estates had sprung up everywhere. Yet coming into the city centre, Vicky was struck by the familiar good-humoured attitude of the Dublin taxi-driver who hummed and whistled amidst eternal gear changes, stops and starts. Then, as the taxi emerged from the worst of the bottle-necks, Vicky experienced a sudden pang of loneliness. In a short while Brian would be getting out, and although his setting up house with an old friend would not mean the termination of a long and loving friendship, it was not going to be an easy break. For twenty years he had been a strong and loyal companion to Vicky. Moreover, as Brian alighted from the taxi, Andrew's tears and embrace spoke the love of a youth for his surrogate father. Vicky was visibly broken hearted, and Brian himself was torn within, though it was a measure of his manhood that he could still act the comforter, reassuring Vicky and Andrew that this parting was less dramatic than it seemed.

The taxi's next stop was Aisling's house in Rathfarnham, from where Aisling had repeatedly written Vicky that a warm welcome awaited her and Andrew any time, but especially so in the present circumstances of Vicky's return. On the way Vicky pointed out her childhood home to Andrew. She was unable to gauge, however, if it had changed over the years, as it was secluded and could not be seen properly from the road. As they passed it, Andrew noticed a shade of sorrow fall on his mother's face, and if he could have read her mind, he might have seen Vicky watching scenes from her childhood flash past her like a rapidly moving video.

Aisling proved the perfect hostess over the next fortnight, and together with her partner, she made Vicky and Andrew very much at home. However, Vicky was only too aware of the urgency that faced her in laying the foundations of a secure future in Dublin, beginning with the need to find her own accommodation. Trusting she was able for this task, she marvelled at the inner strength she clearly must have possessed to tear herself away from Dublin twenty years before—only to return now in no more settled circumstances. Yet if Vicky had disliked the prospect of losing Brian's precious daily company and support, it was not that alone which troubled her. Indeed she knew that leaving

Johannesburg had also signalled the onset of Andrew's independence, and that she must stand back and allow him to fend for himself.

ATTENDANCE at the Royal College of Surgeons was a most significant event for Andrew. Indeed it marked his formal entry into manhood, and that same October he moved into a southside Dublin house which he shared with two South African psychology students, who themselves were studying at Trinity College.

So proud of her son at this important juncture, Vicky would have given her life itself to have Hugh now, to be able to look upon his proud, handsome face as he watched Andrew march into the realm of full maturity. Indeed similarly painful thoughts had haunted her throughout her years in South Africa. No one could fault the goodness and loyalty of Brian, but Vicky still had often imagined how Hugh might have fathered Andrew. Perhaps the most dreadful hours of her life had been spent gazing at her new-born son and wishing, like one demented, that Hugh might suddenly appear. The same longing had always persisted, but it recurred with a greater intensity at special times, such as Andrew's birthdays, his first day starting school, or his first rugby match, not to mention Christmas which always sounded its own sad chorus of loneliness and longing.

Although Andrew loved the ambience of the College of Surgeons, he also spent a lot of time with his new-found friends in Trinity College. One of his former teachers at Daleside College had graduated there, and Andrew had heard much about its history and customs. If in South Africa he had wondered what it must have been like when Wolfe Tone or Robert Emmett studied in its hallowed halls, here in Dublin he could actually stop to view at leisure the Book of Kells, a page of which was daily turned. Attending Commons, he was similarly intrigued by the recitation of Grace in Latin, a custom that had survived the centuries.

What's more, Andrew was delighted to find such a varied social life in Dublin, where he could enjoy a pint in comfort amid the obvious friendliness of both barmen and customers. The night-club scene was also lively, and Vicky enjoyed hearing of Andrew's exploits. If he got to know the ropes rather quickly, she was pleased that he occasionally visited the theatre and the National Concert Hall too!

It was in one of her house-hunting weeks that Vicky found herself gazing at her own former home. The general lay-out of the garden was the same, and it was obvious that great care went into its upkeep. The owner, who could have been her mother trowelling a little patch as Vicky approached, kindly showed her around the house, yet for all her kindness, Vicky felt an undeniable feeling of resentment. However, she was grateful for the cup of tea, and an ear to listen to her memories of the house. What's more, she drove away with a heightened sense of time gone by, having learned that her host had reared two daughters in that bungalow, one married in Canada, the other having moved into a modern apartment near Christchurch.

Vicky's dream was to buy a quiet cottage, and she had in fact saved enough money in South Africa to buy a modest dwelling. The opportunity arose when an elderly couple decided to move closer to the city, and although some repairs needed to be carried out, their cottage at the foot of the Dublin mountains was a bargain she could not refuse.

A month after moving in, Vicky plucked up the courage to re-read another chapter of her life. Indeed it seemed Howth held its breath that evening as she looked at the quiet sea, remembering glorious days of sunshine bobbing on the gentle waves. The *Sea Scamp* was gone, of course, a more sophisticated craft now in its mooring place.

The hill walk was wearying, but she felt she had to do it. Only once did she reach out for a familiar hand, only to grasp the evening air. Still, she could almost hear Hugh's well-modulated voice pointing out various flowers and birdlife. It seemed like only yesterday when she had shown him the dolmen which, as she explained, marked the grave of Aideen who died of grief at the loss of her husband Oscar, never thinking then of what she might come to share with Aideen.

Reaching the house, she saw the plaque bearing the name Seagrave was gone. The garden fountain was also silent and a string of greenish slime hung from its two tiers. Vicky stared in disbelief at the curtained windows and the *For Sale* sign. How could any owner wish to sell? One night of love alone in this grand house had given her a reason to live, and for Vicky this sacred home could never be a mere property on the market!

Staring at the silent Abbey Tavern, too early for its merrymakers, Vicky's head filled once more with the words of that one ballad: "I wish I was in Carrickfergus, ah for one night of love in Carrick grand, I would swim over the deepest ocean, the deepest ocean my love to find. But the sea is wide, and I can't swim over, and neither have I wings to fly." She could see Hugh so clearly — his lovely smile, his manly grace, his look of boyish amusement as he surveyed the happy crowd, before bringing his gaze back to her, transfixing her with eyes that spoke of his enjoyment and deep love.

Vicky did not sleep that night. At one point when she seemed to doze off, she thought she felt a warm and gentle arm encircling her. The brutal reality was her utter solitude, however, and that reality banished all hope of sleep. Wide awake, she lay wondering where Hugh was now? If only God could grant her the miracle of just hearing his voice.

Once more she fell into the misty realm where sleep and wakefulness merge, only this time to sense the outlines of a dream. A frenzied auctioneer was rapping his gavel and she could see he was determined in his business, as he sang out the ascending bid prices. A revolving pole with hundreds of *For Sale* signs spun round at great speed. Once more awake, she realised her visit to Seagrave had only stirred her memories afresh. As dawn delivered her once more from the lonely dark, she accepted this was the price she had to pay for having attempted to gaze at a past that might have been. Yet were she to truly drain her chalice of suffering, that greater purification might just free her from future turmoil, though it might also utterly undermine her very existence.

Still, anything would be better than hobbling around chained to a past which threatened such delirium as she had known this night. And so she decided to see once more the interior of Seagrave House — at whatever risk.

As the estate agent replaced the phone, he felt in much better form. Business had been slow, but here was a potential buyer, one who seemed to have a clear idea of her requirements and of the asking price that would be involved. Nor was it very often that a property so well appointed as Seagrave came on the market. He glanced with approval at the many compelling selling-points he had prepared. Yes, this viewer could be exactly what was required, a doctor interested in investing in a quiet, secluded property.

From the moment the auctioneer opened the gate for Vicky, he saw that the garden with its rapidly cleaned fountain had made its impression on her. Yet Vicky hardly heard him comment on how spacious the property was, addressing her once again as Dr Vaughan. If Vicky felt guilty, it was only a tiny white lie that might just free her from the phantoms now daily haunting her. A shrewd business man, the estate agent was not inexperienced in dealing with experts in his own field, and he was usually quick to endorse any sign of approval that a potential buyer might show, such as the way Vicky fingered the antique mahogany table in the hallway. However, his remarks now fell on deaf ears, and he watched uneasily as Vicky gazed at the long gold-framed mirror, noting a reflection that vaguely disturbed him, a face of exquisite beauty, whose eyes now winced at some hidden cruelty of life.

Unbidden, Vicky walked into the parlour. Several changes had been made over the years, but the piano still stood in its accustomed place of honour. True, it was an old and valuable piano, but what was it that caused his client to stare at it as if possessed? And what moved her to lift the keyboard top, and press a finger on the ivory, causing a middle C to echo through the room?

Duty demanded that he point out the excellent extras still attached to the property, due to the untimely death of the late owner, but the confused auctioneer just could not concentrate; in fact, his better judgement told him to stand aside. He could not say how he knew this doctor had her own agenda, but he thought it best not to follow her upstairs, whatever his colleagues would have made of such gentlemanly deference. Had he followed Vicky, he would have seen her face turn pale with grief as she stood at the open door of the master bedroom. He would have next seen her gaze at its bed, then move to a bookshelf near the window. He would have seen her trembling hand move along the contemporary paperbacks, until it came to a hardback volume. He would have been alarmed to see her open it, stare at the signature on the inside cover, then fall to the bed with heaving sobs.

For Vicky, the hand-written name of Doctor Hugh Osbourne Burke had seemed to leap up from the page, challenging her disbelief. Obviously Hugh had forgotten the book, nor had the new owner bothered to shift it. Torn between her desire to keep the volume, and a mortal fear of the pain it might provoke, Vicky struggled within, knowing that his handwriting would only serve as an agonising reminder of a night when heaven and earth were one. She remembered that very night when she had chuckled at his shyness, trying not to laugh at his two pillows, the books piled at the foot of his bed, the open drawers, the pipe leaning against the beside lamp, before surrendering herself to the keen edge of her passion. Clutching the book, she pressed it to her face, which now streamed with tears. Then, her body shaking uncontrollably, she slowly replaced it. Visibly shaken, her reappearance downstairs confirmed for the estate agent that his client had far more interest in this property than met the eye. If still mystified when she drove off in the waiting taxi, there was no way he could know of the thunderously violent impact the sight of that bedroom had visited on her. Clearly her sacred pilgrimage to Seagrave had failed to take her beyond her memories and her grief.

THE miserable weather of Christmas Eve a month later did not prevent a festive spirit from descending on Grafton Street. Carol singers sang their hearts out in spite of the numbing sleet. One little chap among them looked especially comical, clearly determined that the higher notes of the First Noël would not defeat him as the elements plastered his curly hair. Buskers a few yards away were competing with ease, their percussions punctuating the wintery air at rapid, sharp intervals. Suddenly Vicky's gaze was arrested by a six-foot-tall, utterly immobile figure in a nearby shop entrance. It was the Dublin master of mime himself, shrouded in stillness, his death-like, waxen face matching his long black cloak in an eerie way. A crowd of amused spectators scrutinised his form, including children both intrigued and somewhat frightened. Each time a coin was thrown into the box at his feet, the donor was rewarded with a practiced wink, though only an eyelid moved.

This Christmas was to be Andrew's first in Ireland, for whom Christmas in South Africa had always been a happy occasion, thanks to Vicky and Brian who had seen to that. And while Vicky did not relish the crop of memories that lurked behind every Dublin Christmas tree and every sprig of holly, she was nonetheless delighted to see Andrew's enthusiasm. This Christmas Eve he was meeting his two South African friends, before joining Vicky and Brian in Davy Byrne's for a festive drink. This evening would be an appropriate warm-up for Christmas Day, when they would all dine together. Meanwhile the carnival of flashing fairy-lights somehow seemed to soften the east wind along Grafton Street. As Vicky passed by, Bewleys' door opened to release a rush of warm air onto the street, carrying with it the rich aroma of coffee and freshly baked bread, making her think of Dickensian chestnuts roasting on red hot coals. Still she pressed on, until she reached the large, elegant windows of Brown Thomas. Was it her absence for twenty years that now enabled her to ever more appreciate the classic, severe design of this old building? Master craftsmen had left their imprint on its magnificent form, its patriarchal character standing in proud defiance of the more frivolous face of modern commerce.

Vicky was well aware of this grandeur, but her interest in Brown Thomas had many other strands, and a surge of overwhelming emotion quickly seized her. Composing herself, she realised the driving wind had ceased its assault, so she clicked her brolly shut and pulled the zip. Standing there for several minutes, she sensed in a strange way that the arrangement in the window of Brown Thomas had worked to both calm and soothe her. Tiny lights flickered all round the edges, enshrining a setting of exquisite taste. Cleverly arranged sprays of silvery light fell on a framed Constable reproduction, to the right of which stood a glistening candelabra. A strikingly rich red scarf, bordered with a soft white rim, lay nearest to the window, and on it rested a snow-white pair of cosy mittens. Further back hung a Ralph Lauren tweed sports coat, a Kapp & Peterson pipe looking out from its top pocket. The window display bore the hallmarks of an expert touch, leading Vicky to wonder if Mr Redmond still worked there? If not, someone else's caring hand had triumphantly reproduced the excellence of twenty years before.

A single step sideways allowed her to peer within. Even the to-ings and fro-ings of the busy throng of last-minute shoppers in the well-heated building did not obscure the staircase that some deep-set quarry had yielded its heart to adorn, its marble steps leading to the downstairs restaurant. Overhead three crystal chandeliers clung to minutely decorated plaster borders. Stepping once more to the side, Vicky undertook the bittersweet task of looking into the cosmetic area. Here the great brand names leapt into her view: Giorgio Beverly Hills, Lancome, Aramis, Estée Lauder, Elizabeth Arden and of course Chanel. It was this latter great French creation that now claimed her attention, and Vicky found herself studying the Chanel girl, a tall, chic type, whose uniform of black skirt and white blouse with gold buttons, obviously suited her. Her courteous efficiency was evident, even from that distance, and her short cropped hair style suggested a perfect mixture of both seriousness and levity. Unbeknownst to the Chanel Girl, her observer was at this moment making a personal comparison. "She has a certain confidence, a certain wisdom perhaps, that I certainly lacked when I was in her shoes," Vicky thought. "But then I hadn't really grown up, nor had the hardships of life moved in yet to dull my own glittering eyes."

She took a last lingering look, failing to see a single familiar face at the cosmetic counters. Guilt and remorse then overtook her as she thought of Louise, Sophie and Sharon. Though she had intended answering their letters, she just could not get beyond the first line or two, for the pain was too much. And so eventually the letters had ceased to arrive. Suddenly Vicky realised that the sleet had started again, the window once more glistening in syrupy layers that shifted the dazzling reflections within.

Moving into the doorway, she scarcely heard the brave refrain of Jingle Bells from the little group of carol singers. Instead, a terrifying undertow threatened to draw her into Brown Thomas, if only to see the spot where she had first glimpsed Hugh. No — she must not, she could not bear the further pain. Besides, Brian and Andrew were probably ensconced in Davy Byrne's by now. Suddenly the door nearest to Vicky sprung open with a sharp "clack." A woman in black emerged hurriedly, then pushed the door back and called out at someone to "hold the fort." Once more the door whooshed closed with a sharp clatter, the woman by now running up to the flower lady a few yards away, as Vicky looked after her in shock. Hadn't Zoë always used that very phrase "Hold the fort" whenever she left the store without permission? Could it possibly be Zoë, whom Vicky had not spotted through the window? What's more, a Zoë whose hair was now blonde? As the woman returned to make a quiet entry, Vicky took a closer look at her. No, she was not mistaken. In turn Zoë almost dropped her bunch of flowers when Vicky, touching her arm, said her name. Breathless from her rapid excursion to the flower-lady, Zoë was now utterly flummoxed.

"Victoria Vaughan! I just don't believe it. I must be seeing things. Vicky, it's great to see you. I'd given up hope of ever laying eyes on you again. Surely this is the best Christmas box I ever got. You certainly left it long enough before visiting us, though. Jesus, this is not for real!" she finally stopped.

Still shaken with surprise, Vicky finally managed, "I'm not long returned from South Africa, Zoë. And it's a long way from Johannesburg to Dublin."

"You mean you never even came home for a holiday, Vicky?"

"No, when I went, I intended staying there. As you know, there were complications..." Drawing a breath, she added, "I didn't think I'd see you here, Zoë?"

"Just doing my usual Christmas stint. They give me a few weeks every year, so far so good. Look, what the hell are we doing out here in the cold? Come on in to my counter."

Vicky started to say that she did not really feel up to it—especially at Christmas time. Before she could utter a word, however, Zoë had pushed open the door with her shoulder, secured her grip on the flowers, and with her free hand dragged Vicky by the wrist, the doors swinging closed behind them both. At first Vicky felt uneasy, but gradually she relaxed as she observed the ease with which Zoë could attend to her customers, then take up the conversation where it had left off.

"Well, Vicky, to tell the truth we did hear that things hadn't worked out so well, but then the talk just fizzled out. Nobody seemed to be corresponding with you, but we respected that such was probably your decision. Anyway, we did hear that you had a son, Vicky, didn't you?"

"Yes, he's been my constant love all these years," Vicky smiled, opening her bag and showing Zoë a photo of Andrew, before proceeding to explain about his getting a place in the College of Surgeons.

"Wowee," gasped Zoë. "Don't I wish I were twenty years younger. He's only gorgeous."

"So, how are things with yourself, Zoë?"

"Well, Vicky, for better or for worse I'm still living with the man who put the ring on me, though at times I think I need my head examined. Still, I suppose he's not a bad ould sort as men go."

She noticed Vicky become slightly uncomfortable, however, and after serving a customer, decided not to dwell on the subject, only to hear Vicky ask if she had any children.

"Two boys, and a girl."

"The years have been kind to you," said Vicky with a genuine smile. "You're still the same Zoë I knew in Mr Klein's time. Is he still here?"

"He certainly is," Zoë laughed, "and as good-looking as ever. God, Vicky, will you ever forget the day he chewed the head off us for sneaking out of the store. I forget what it was about, but I'll never forget being expelled for the week over it."

"I couldn't forget it either," Vicky laughed. "That was the second time for me to stand in his office. You remember when I threw the book?" As both women laughed again, Zoë was pleased to see Vicky relaxing into better form. At that moment, Rachel Sweeney, still the Personnel Manager, happened to cross the floor. She stopped dead in her tracks, however, when she saw Vicky, and it took her some time to recover after confirming that it was indeed the Chanel Girl of so many years ago.

"And what are you doing with yourself at the moment," she asked Vicky after several minutes of a heart-to-heart chat with both women.

After Vicky explained her present circumstances, Rachel offered with a smile, "We're looking for part-time staff in our new store."

"That's it over there," Rachel pointed across the road. "The new Brown Thomas," she added proudly.

Looking over, Vicky noticed some of the scaffolding still standing along the face of the fine-looking building. "Sure, I'd love to apply, but it's been so long," she finally replied, her face a welter of conflicting emotions."

"Hush!" said Rachel. "Maybe you haven't had your hand in practice for some time, but one look at you would tell you're still an expert on the old grooming, and you haven't lost your figure either! I used to envy you, Victoria Vaughan! Look, wait here, and I'll get you an application form just for the formalities."

She left Zoë and Vicky, humming as she strode towards the office. And before Vicky left, Zoë insisted on an exchange of telephone numbers, declaring that another twenty year's wait would be out of the question!

Vicky sensed a new lightness to her step as she headed for Davy Byrne's. Joining Andrew and Brian, she told them about her prospective new job, but added in a more serious voice, "I'm in two minds about it, though. I don't know if I could fit into the cosmetic world again, never mind that it holds so many memories." Sensing the excitement in her voice, however, Andrew and Brian encouraged her in a positively light-hearted way, and by the evening's end they were quietly confident they had succeeded.

THE unexpectedly happy Christmas and New Year celebrations seemed to make time fly. Shortly after Vicky decided to take up her official appointment as part-time cosmetic lady in the new Brown Thomas, and as it happened her first duties were to assist at the official opening night.

When the night finally arrived, it seemed fitting that she should be resuming employment in a completely new environment. Whatever sentimental attachments still lived within her for the old premises quickly began to fade with the thought of both the new premises and her new beginning. It even gave her a certain courage that a new era in her life was underway. The whole premises had a marvellous air of freshness, abetted by floral arrangements which added a pristine atmosphere to the whole proceedings, and more than one individual cascade of assorted flowers invited closer inspection. What's more, Vicky's positive feelings were further reinforced by the sight of a host of VIPs with their personal bodyguards wearing identity tabs. The gentlemen were distinguished by their perfectly fitting dark suits, and the ladies by their fashionable dresses, shirts and hats.

Of course, some things never changed, and there working alongside Vicky was Zoë, just as she had been years ago. In fact, it was Zoë who drew Vicky's attention to the arrival of Galen Weston and his beautiful wife, Hilary. Vicky was mesmerised, for he was still as handsome, if not even more distinguished. While his arrival evoked her day-dreams of earlier years, a swift glance at the lovely Hilary told Vicky that a fairy-tale romance had been realised in no uncertain fashion.

The evening seemed to fly by, thanks to the heavy traffic of customers, as well as the constant procession of impressed onlookers. It was not until a quarter hour before closing time that Vicky and Zoë had time for a chat, as they surveyed the magic scene with interest. "Ah Vicky, just look at all those MTs and YTs," Zoë said with a laugh.

Vicky smiled upon hearing the secret codes of yesteryears, the hours spent discussing the "my types" and "your types". Suddenly Zoë spoke again,

"Vicky, Galen Weston is heading this way with a real MT!"

Vicky turned to look but so abrupt was her movement that a display bottle of perfume fell to the floor. It spilt its fragrance, and within seconds the air was drenched with its heavy richness. One girl pushed the other in a frantic effort to save the situation, fearing Galen Weston would just freak! Unable to restrain their giggling, they almost fell over each other, as the two men neared the counter. While Zoë tried to remedy the matter with a handful of tissues, Vicky pretended to be tidying the lowest shelf, so that to passers-by they were invisible, including Galen Weston and his companion who were now within speaking distance.

"You say you remember our old store?" both girls heard Galen Weston inquire.

"Yes indeed," his companion answered, "it held very special memories for me."

Crouched below her counter, Vicky froze in shock, certain that she recognised that voice. Could it possibly be...? Or was it only the heavy fragrance deluding her? She listened again with suspended breath, waiting for what seemed an eternity.

"Well, Dr Hugh," Galen Weston spoke again, "I hope you enjoyed your evening." Before his companion had a chance to answer, a stunned and disbelieving Vicky straightened up from behind her counter and stared wide-eyed, managing only to call out "Hugh."

For his part Galen Weston feared Dr Hugh was suffering a heart attack, as the veins of his neck and temples leapt into relief, and beads of perspiration broke out on his forehead. Meanwhile the champagne glass he had been holding slipped from his fingers and shattered at his feet. His lips moved in rapid succession as if he were frantically trying to speak, yet all he could stammer was, "This is not real — it cannot be," as he squeezed Galen Weston's arm in the vice-like grip of the truly deranged.

"Christ, I think I'm losing my mind," he finally whispered. "Is that really you, Vicky?" At that, his eyes suddenly swamped, as though a torrent had been unleashed from his very core. Effectively blinded, it took some moments before he could refocus on Vicky, never mind loosen the strangling bonds that prevented any further speech.

If Galen Weston's first shock was considerable, it was nothing compared to the drama that now unfolded before him as Hugh and Vicky locked in a speechless embrace for what seemed to Vicky another small eternity. When conversation became possible again, Hugh urged Vicky to adjourn to the Brown Thomas restaurant. He didn't have to persuade for very long; however before leaving, Vicky turned to her stunned co-worker and asked, "Would you do me a favour,

Zoë? Would you mind calling to Davy Byrne's to tell Andrew I'll be late? He expected me to go in straight after the closing." Distracted, Vicky did not even wait for a reply, as Hugh took her hand in his and led her away.

Meanwhile Zoë own thoughts raced at high speed as she made her way to the pub, where she quickly spotted Andrew to whom Vicky had introduced her some days previously. Spying an empty stool beside Andrew, she fell onto it with little ceremony, scarcely hearing Andrew introduce Brian and two other companions, both his flat-mates who were studying psychology at Trinity. All three men were quietly amused at Zoë's efforts to gather her wits, until finally she managed, "You know, I've seen it all! There am I, trying to clean up the remains of a fifty pound bottle of Giorgio Beverly Hills perfume, when I look round to see Vicky wrapped in the arms of one of the finest MTs I ever laid eyes on. Mind you, a bit old for me, but Vicky was always keen on the more senior hunks."

Drawing a breath, Zoë puzzled at their laughter, which was directed as much at the way she spoke as at what she said. She steadied up somewhat, however, when offered a brandy. Agreeing that a large one would not go amiss, she then delivered the most important part of what she had intended to convey. "Anyway, Vicky said she'll be late. Mind you, if what I saw is anything to go by, she'll be very late indeed." With that, Zoë made quick work of the brandy, thanked her amazed company and left the happy gathering to resume their prior conversation.

"What a character," laughed Robin, the taller of the two psychology students.

"Not at all like your mother, Andrew," added Keith, the other student. "Though let's face it, it sounds as if your mom still enjoys the odd romance! Is she also working in Brown Thomas tonight?"

"Yes," replied a bemused Andrew. "She's looking after the VIPs for the official opening."

"I think Ossie got an invitation to that," Robin idly remarked, at which Andrew looked even more puzzled.

"You remember my telling you about Ossie, the American psychology professor?" Keith added. "It seems he's very well got in Dublin social circles, having lived here once before. Mind you, he's something of a brain-box, having published a mountain of books."

"So what brought him back to Ireland?" Andrew asked.

"Oh, I suppose being offered a professorship in psychology at Trinity had something to do with it," Robin laughed. "Strange, though, my father worked for a time in Florida where Ossie also lived, and he reckons, from what he heard there, that Ossie left Dublin years ago over a broken love affair."

"But why do you call him Aussie if he's not Australian?" Andrew asked.

"Ossie, not Aussie," laughed Keith. "It's from his middle name, Osbourne. Besides, Ossie is less of a mouthful than Dr Hugh Osbourne Burke!"

Neither of the South African students noticed Andrew's nor Brian's stunned expression as they continued chattering in a light-hearted manner. Finally a thunderstruck Brian broke his own silence, "Well, it didn't take you guys long to acquire a taste for Guinness, never mind find a pub which deserves its reputation for a decent pint." And holding up his nearly empty glass, he pointed to the thick coating of creamy froth that still clung to its sides.

THE restaurant at Brown Thomas was crowded, yet the determined waitress had already made three trips to one of her tables. On the first occasion she knew it was hopeless, as she took in the constant hand-clasping, the muted cries of joy and the fact that no obvious effort was being made by either Hugh or Vicky to read the menu. The second effort was equally fruitless, as the two were still too breathless and excited to order. The third time proved lucky however, though only two cups of coffee were ordered.

After the waitress departed, a more sombre Hugh spoke.

"Is Andrew, who I heard you say is waiting in Davy Byrne's, your husband, Vicky? And tell me — I suppose there's family?"

Vicky heard so clearly how he delivered every word, questioning her in the gentlest, most deliberate way possible. Determined to immediately rescue him from any further agony, her hand once more covered his.

"No Hugh — there has never been anyone else in my life. And how about you?" she inquired in turn, feeling as if she were treading a mine-field, but knowing the question had to be asked.

"Jesus, Vicky," Hugh spoke with difficulty, "I've known some hard things in my life, but the worst task I ever faced was writing that 'letter of release' to you. It drove me to the verge of suicide, Vicky — and I was supposed to be a psychiatrist, a pillar of strength! Good God — it was to be only a page, but I stared at the blank notepaper for days. How I did it I will never know, though I realised our age difference — and nothing on this earth could alter that. In any case, to answer your question, Barbara left after three years, and ever since I've been quite alone."

His voice was breaking now, so Vicky placed a finger on his lips, as one would stop a child from speaking. She did not find it as easy to steady her own voice, though, as she explained to Hugh that the issue of the years between them had actually been her ploy to allow him re-unite with Barbara. Yet only when she informed him that Andrew was in fact his own son, did Vicky realise that the Brown Thomas restaurant was perhaps not the best place to have broken such news. As Hugh placed his hands on his forehead, his broad shoulders shuddered so much the table creaked. His silent convulsions only made Vicky wish she could hold him, soothe him. The coffee grew cold and eventually another two cups arrived, before either Hugh or Vicky felt they possessed the necessary composure for going on to Davy Byrne's.

Pausing outside the pub, Vicky held Hugh's face in both her hands. Looking into his still moist eyes, she assured him that Andrew would be gloriously happy to be formally introduced. Nor could the din from the merrymakers in that popular venue diminish the sacredness of the moment when father and son embraced. Words simply would not come, but the intensity of their meeting was evident. If Brian was still in shock, Andrew's two companions were totally lost, and Vicky was completely overcome. The busy barman eyed the scene, experience telling him that this vignette was something more than the average family reunion! Intrigued, he gathered it was a father and son who stood weeping unashamedly, but he could not quite fathom the reason for the constant embracing and general unabandoned affection between Brian and Hugh, as the latter repeatedly stepped back to replace his arm around Andrew's shoulders. Still dumbstruck, Andrew's companions were all the same very moved by the unfolding drama.

It was late by the time the couple had left the other three in the pub. Pausing at the window of Brown Thomas, Vicky wondered if she was losing her mind, and if all this was, in fact, really happening. Was it truly Hugh who was holding her hand? Indeed his handsome profile had changed little, though she noticed as she ran her fingers through his hair, that a thinning had begun. For his part, Hugh again and again bathed Vicky in his admiring gaze, unaware of the almost unbearable intensity with which he stared into her eyes, as if he wanted to search her very soul.

Utterly tongue-tied, he drew Vicky once more into his warm, protective arms. When at last he could speak, his words seemed to catch in a throat still tight with powerful emotion:

"My God, Vicky, I've been walking Grafton Street everyday at lunchtime since I returned, and there wasn't a moment that I didn't think of you."

They huddled together at the window, conscious only of each other's closeness, and entirely oblivious to the biting wind which threw light traces of sleet along the glass. Vicky felt a shudder ripple through Hugh's frame, and looking up, she saw that while his eyes were tightly closed, tears escaped his eyelids. Squeezing Vicky's hand, he whispered:

"Oh God, what a fool I've been, Vicky. I should never have let you out of my sight. Not only have I tortured myself, but I've caused you dreadful pain." His voice faltered as a sob caught in his throat.

"By Christ, Vicky, if I'd known you were expecting Andrew, there's no way Barbara would ever have got her way."

Vicky's hand slipped inside Hugh's gaberdine and jacket to encircle his waist. Close to tears herself, she somehow held them back.

"I was lost," Hugh continued. "I had lost my son — I had lost my wife. Everything was lost and then I found you. Then what do I do? I lose you for twenty years Not very clever, eh? You were everything to me, Vicky — you are everything to me. Not for a single day did I forget you."

"Is this all real, Hugh?" Vicky finally spoke. "Or am I having a cruel, cruel dream, or am I just going mad?"

Tears of joy mixed with the icy rain that now washed their faces. They heard footsteps, as two Gardai on foot patrol passed by, wishing them "Goodnight."

While that brief encounter convinced Vicky that she was not dreaming, it prompted Hugh to turn to her, still holding her close as though fearful she would slip away and out of his life again. With one arm around her waist, and his other hand holding both of hers, he murmured in a voice still affected by deep emotion, "Is it really you? Is it really you here now in my arms? I cannot believe that after all of these empty years, I've found you again."

Holding her even tighter, he whispered, "Now listen closely to me because I will not let you go again — you're staying with me tonight at my apartment in Mount Merrion. You can send for any things you need in the morning, but I've lost you once and I'm not going to let you out of my sight..."

As they passed through the electronic gates at Mount Merrion, Vicky felt in an inexplicable way that she was coming home, albeit home to an apartment she had yet to see. When Hugh opened the door into the sitting room, Vicky took in the bookish bachelor furnishings: his pipes, scientific journals, the rather shabby, but clearly comfortable, leather chairs and sofa, taking in also the slightly unkempt look that cried out for a quick flick or two of a duster, a plumped up cushion and, no doubt about it some hoovering also. Hugh caught the appraising look in her eyes and laughed, "I know, I know, it's not as it should be, but frankly I just haven't cared. Living alone has meant it's simply been a place to keep my things, to sleep, work and, yes, occasionally drink too much. But now everything will be different because with you I do care, and I want you to have a home you can be proud of..."

Breaking off, he waltzed her about the room. "Stuffy old Professor Burke has gone and the Campus's happiest couple, Dr and Mrs Burke will be in residence." Stopping, he asked Vicky directly, "Will you share my life? Please tell me that you too are as excited and happy as I am? That we're together again and this time we shall stay together?"

Vicky's face spoke volumes, as she laughed at Hugh's boyish delight at the life he envisioned for both of them in the years ahead.

"Come now," she said. "First things first. Such as where are we going to sleep tonight?"

The room fell suddenly quiet as Hugh absorbed Vicky's remark, stopping at the half-opened door to what was evidently a bedroom. With an anxious tone in his voice, he asked, "Vicky, my darling, you will marry me, won't you, and soon? I'm sorry if I've almost bullied you but I must know. You are so important to me that I could not bear it if you are having second thoughts about taking me on. An ageing professor I may be, yes, but one who loves you truly with all his heart, and who wants to make up for our lost years. Too many of them, I know, but trust me, the best is yet to be."

Vicky regarded the undeniably anxious face that awaited her answers. Her confident and authoritative Hugh, used to making decisions and being obeyed, now stood clearly uncertain, clearly fearful of anything less than a whole-hearted reply.

After a few moment's reflection that to Hugh seemed endless, Vicky said nothing, but dropping her coat over a chair, moved forward and took Hugh's hand, leading him into the bedroom where a simple bedside table lamp revealed a frugally furnished room with a single bed. Putting her fingers on his lips, Vicky pulled the duvet and pillows onto the floor and tenderly started to undo the buttons on Hugh's shirt. As the meaning of her movements sank in, Hugh reached for Vicky and held her close.

"Thank you, thank you for making me the happiest man in Dublin, in Ireland, in, oh hell, anywhere, damn it!" His lips pressed on hers as they clung to each other, then without a word their clothes gradually fell away, interrupted only by the frequent embraces that spoke their pent-up feelings.

Calmer now, Hugh luxuriated in touching the woman he so adored. Gently, tenderly, he caressed Vicky with hands that trembled with desire, and Vicky's kisses became more urgent as their naked bodies touched, moved away, then touched again.

The night passed only too quickly, and it was not until just before dawn that they fell asleep in each other's arms. Awakening, they embraced again, then rose from the floor with aching limbs, yet feeling curiously rested, as they laughed at their unsatiable frenzy of the previous night.

Stretching on tip-toe, Vicky blushed as she remembered the intensity of her desire. "Professor Burke," she declared, "the first thing we must do is get a double bed." Hugh laughed aloud, "Anything you say, my darling, but please let's have breakfast first, I'm starving."

WASHING up their breakfast dishes, Vicky mentally prepared a list of what must be done before moving into Hugh's Merrion apartment. Behind her, she could hear Hugh phoning Andrew to confirm that they would meet outside the Royal College of Surgeons after the afternoon lecture.

Once at Brown Thomas, it came as no surprise to hear Zoë giggling at her shoulder and rolling her eyes as she peeked at the underwear Vicky was quickly buying before starting work in the cosmetics area.

"So come on, tell me, who didn't go home last night and why not? And who in God's name was the YT whose arms were squeezing the life out of you?"

As always, Vicky instantly lost her composure, and soon they were both giggling almost hysterically as Vicky said, "It was Hugh, Zoë, my Hugh, from so long ago, and he still wants me! Isn't that wonderful? And he likes Andrew, loves Andrew — well, he will do, I'm sure." The words tumbled out, and as the cosmetics supervisor turned a friendly blind eye, Vicky talked herself almost hoarse, telling Zoë of the reunion with Hugh and that of Andrew with his father. "We can make it work, Zoë," Vicky finally finished up, "I know we can."

"Well," said Zoë, feeling more than a little envious, "I can see from your staff discount voucher that you haven't let the grass grow under your feet!"

Blushing, Vicky admitted that she'd spent the night with Hugh, hence her purchases. Still she had no regrets. "Zoë, I could not be without him again, I feel I'd waited so long that I just could not spend another night alone. We do love each other, and very soon we will be married at the Registry Office on Kildare Street. Please say you will be with us? So many people have been kind to me over the past years that I want to share my happiness with the entire world."

"Humph," said Zoë, "the whole world wouldn't fit into the Registry Office! But yes, of course I'll be there, provided you get a Church blessing," she laughed, "and we have lots to drink afterwards — bubbly I trust!"

At that very moment Hugh was strolling through St Stephen's Green marshalling his thoughts as he came to terms with the new direction his life was to take. After a brisk circumference of the Green's inner paths, he found his mind made up, and leaving by the main gate he hailed a cab, instructing the driver, "Howth Harbour as quick as you can, as I've lots to do and little enough time."

Later that afternoon, Andrew was wondering if perhaps something was amiss as the clock showed a quarter past four outside the College of Surgeons. Suddenly he spied a flustered Dr Hugh push through a crowd of Japanese tourists cluttered with cameras and guidebooks, and cross the road.

"Sorry, Andrew, I did so want to be on time," he apologised. "I know how tired you must be after a day's lectures, but I've had a lot to do and precious little time to spare. Anyway I've had a good day and I hope you have too, but more about that later. Let's go and have a drink at McDaids? " Clearly nervous, Hugh barely drew a breath before continuing. "I'm meeting your mother later for dinner, however we've got lots to talk about — in fact we've got years of talking to catch up on. After all it's not every day that I find I'm the father of a young man who has already accomplished so much. But first let me repeat what I said last night. I do regret intensely I was not there when you needed a father, and to share in your growing up. I have lost out, not being with you, yet if you felt bitter about what you thought had been an absentee father, apparently disinterested and making no effort to find you, I'd understand."

"No, no!" protested Andrew. "How could I be bitter if you never knew of my birth? Besides, my mother had explained the circumstances of her leaving Ireland. Her love certainly prevented me from feeling unwanted — and, of course, Brian was always there when we needed him. Not my father perhaps, but a good friend to mother and my idea of a perfect uncle. So put that thought right out of your head. I feel regret, yes, for what might have been, but bitter — certainly not!"

After this anxious and somewhat stilted beginning, Hugh and Andrew quickly warmed to each other and, finding so much in common, both men freely accepted that their futures would be inextricably linked. Just before they parted, Hugh to meet Vicky and Andrew to study, Hugh placed his hands on Andrew's shoulders and asked for his help.

"Andrew, we are a very new father and son team, and I know it's early to be asking for favours, but your mother and I are marrying next week, and I want to arrange a special party at the Abbey Tavern in Howth on the night before. Vicky has spoken so warmly of her friends here in Dublin, as well as Sharon in London, and I want as many as possible to be our guests. You know some of them, and those you do not know will be known to Zoë, so please, might you ask as many as possible if they would honour us by sharing a very special occasion?"

"Money does not matter," he continued, "so make sure that where transport is required or costs involved, no one is to be out of pocket. Let's have her friends from Brown Thomas, as they are such a grand crowd and I know Vicky feels indebted to them for the warm friendship they have so freely given her."

"But remember discretion," Hugh cautioned. "I want this night to be a surprise Vicky will never forget. So I'm relying on you, Andrew, and I am not forgetting Brian either. I owe him so much for all the years he looked after you and Vicky." At that, after exchanging a quick hug, the two men went their separate ways, Hugh with a spring in his step, and Andrew with clearly much to think about.

VICKY smiled in the darkness of the car as Hugh drove to pick up Andrew for what she assumed would be a quiet family dinner. She fingered her lovely sapphire earrings, and felt the matching necklace move on her breast. These treasured gifts of yesteryear, so reminiscent of a shattered love, and so long unworn thanks to their bittersweet memories, were now the perfect adornment for a night such as this. Nor was Vicky unaware of how they complemented her Cartier watch whose face was ringed with matching gems.

Suddenly, turning in her seat, she asked, "Hugh, could we do one thing before we collect Andrew? It won't take the whole night."

Hugh listened with the slightest hesitation before consenting. "It would be wonderful, Vicky," he nodded, "to revive such happy memories."

Ten minutes later Vicky found herself staring at Seagrave House with a lump in her throat. Hugh was also obviously moved, though neither of them left the car to view the stately residence. Nevertheless, Vicky was able to see a great deal from the passenger's side. The gate was the same gate she had walked through years before, and the two solid glass net-weights still sat atop their pillars. Clearly neglected for some time, the garden showed some recent signs of being restored towards its former beauty, and the two-tiered fountain in the centre once again overflowed with clear water.

Vicky's eyes wandered from the *Sold* sign up to the windows swathed in lavishly plush fawn curtains. Her gaze rested for a moment on the window of the bedroom in which she had known her first moments of heaven on earth, then returned again to the estate agent's sign.

"It's a horrible feeling, Hugh, looking at that sign. I remember when I first came back here, I felt so angry at seeing Seagrave was for sale. It's the feeling you'd get if a burglar broke into your house—as if it's no longer really your own."

"I know that feeling so well," Hugh sighed, "I know it so well. Anyway, I think we'd better make tracks now to collect Andrew. Don't want to have him waiting."

Kissing her on the cheek, he started the car. Vicky briefly puzzled over his lack of emotion on re-visiting Seagrave, finally putting it down to his habit of keeping his hurt to himself. It seemed in many ways that Hugh hadn't changed a great deal!

Having collected Andrew who was waiting at the Howth Dart station, they went swiftly to the Abbey Tavern, where the genial hostess ushered them to a discreet table on the ground floor with a lovely floral arrangement linking the three set places. After pre-dinner drinks were served, Hugh called the waiter over and asked, raising his voice above the loud ballad music, if it were possible to have a table upstairs instead. "Since we're celebrating a quiet family occasion," he explained, "the merry carnival atmosphere here sounds a bit too much."

"No problem at all, sir," the waiter assured him, "just wait a few minutes for the table decorations to be transferred, and you can proceed upstairs."

Their drinks finished, Vicky led the way upstairs to the main function room. As they arrived, Andrew opened the door with a flourish, and Hugh took Vicky's elbow and gently eased her a step forward. It was a faltering step, however, which came to a halt at the laughing welcome that swelled forth from a room full of smiling faces. Faces of friends from far and wide, all happy to share in her joy and chorusing their congratulations.

When she had partially recovered her composure, Vicky, still in tears, falteringly thanked them for their good wishes, then toasted them in turn. At that Hugh stepped forward, and putting his arm around Vicky's waist, asked for their indulgence while he spoke a few words.

Lifting Vicky's hand, he spoke of the honour Vicky was to do him by becoming his wife. He described his real pleasure in also gaining a son as well as a wife and that, in truth, his cup was indeed running over. He added that he had a lot of catching up to do for the nearly twenty years that had elapsed since he'd been in Dublin, and as his voice broke, a quick toast was proposed to the happy couple.

Turning then to Brian, "to whom I will always be indebted," Hugh asked him to bring forward a package, gaily wrapped and with a multi-coloured bow, which Brian lifted from a small side-table. Placing the package in Vicky's hands, Hugh kissed her, saying, "Darling, we have missed so much together that we must make the most of whatever time the good Lord will grant us."

Slowly unwrapping it in the hushed room, Vicky stared at a beautiful Celtic-lettered bronze plaque, inscribed *Seagrave House*, from which hung a silver house key on a silken cord.

Vicky could feel the blood draining from her head as she struggled not to pass out. As if from a great distance, she heard Hugh speaking to her.

"I almost gave the game away a few hours ago, Vicky, as we sat looking at Seagrave House. Every nerve-ending in me burned as I watched you look so longingly at the house, and I could see the past being rekindled in your eyes."

Pausing to wipe his eyes, Hugh smiled at her. "I've been a bold boy these past few days, Vicky, and I know you've wondered once or twice where I've been. The answer is that I was making arrangements to purchase Seagrave, and I closed the deal yesterday."

If the onlookers witnessed a sobbing Vicky clinging to her Hugh's shoulders, they shed their share of tears too. Running his hands through her hair, Hugh coaxed her ear towards his mouth and whispered, "We'll go there in a short while, darling." There was little need to whisper, as the room fairly resounded with a chorus of excited voices. But those nearest to the couple could hear Hugh add with a laugh, "Welcome home, Vicky, welcome home."